Meredith's Treasure

PHILIP HARBOTTLE

A Black Horse Western

ROBERT HALE · L NDON

To my favourite author,
E. C. Tubb
and my favourite granddaughter,
Eleanor Rose King

Typeset by
Derek Doyle & Associates, Liverpool.
Printed and bound in Great Britain by
Antony Rowe Limited, Wiltshire

Meredith's Treasure

An amazing discovery in the mountains leads to some very odd events in the little Arizona town of Mountain Peak. When a man is found dead on the mountain trail – the dust around his body undisturbed by footprints, no signs of external injury or indication of how he died – it's left to Mayor Randle Meredith to provide some answers.

Aided by his son, courageous young wife, June, their enigmatic Navajo servant and the town sheriff, Randle is quickly faced with two more inexplicable deaths.

Now, Randle's battle to protect his town from a murderer leaves him fighting desperately for his very life.

1

UNEXPECTED VISITORS

Mountain Peak seemed almost asleep – a sweltering little township in the shadow of impersonal mountains, soaking in the torrid Arizona sunlight until every board was warped, and every trace of paint had been blistered. Few had the energy – especially during the summer – to do any repairs. The inhabitants of Mountain Peak were apparently content to drowse the grilling hours away.

In was mid-afternoon. Hardly a figure moved on the boardwalks, or came in and out of the buildings; no buckboards and teams were in sight on the dusty main street. And since the Painted Lady saloon was closed until the evening, even this gin-palace looked dead.

One exception to the inactivity was the sheriff – Bart Meredith, working in his office behind drawn shades. Since he had only recently taken over the job, there was much to do, particularly neglected paperwork. Bart was young, dark-haired, with blue eyes and a determined jaw. He was unusual in that he was an educated man, reared in

Boston – ex-playboy turned into Westerner, and now as fast on the draw as anyone.

Bart looked up at the click of the latch on his office door. Who on earth could wish to see him in the middle of a blazing afternoon? Footsteps sounded behind the partition, then a small, inoffensive-looking figure came into the office.

The visitor was dressed in dusty black, a wide-brimmed hat, and – most surprisingly – with a dog collar encircling his thin neck.

'Good afternoon, Sheriff,' he said, smiling.

Bart nodded politely. The man was a complete stranger to him. From his dusty attire he had ridden a considerable distance; and his lack of gun holsters was perhaps explained by his spiritual calling. He had a pink face, grey eyes, and white hair showed under the sides of his black hat.

'I am the Reverend Maurice Peregrine,' he explained, almost apologetically. 'I have my headquarters in Nebraska.'

'Headquarters?' Brad asked vaguely.

'I am *the* Peregrine, Sheriff. The creator of the Reformed Sinners' Gospel.'

'Afraid I'm none the wiser, Reverend,' Bart smiled faintly. 'But have a seat, anyway. What can I do for you?'

The clergyman sat in the chair Bart indicated, removing his broad-brimmed hat to reveal white hair with a centre parting.

'I assume, Sheriff, that you are the right man to ask about accommodation in this town? I am touring many of the small backwoods towns of Arizona – and hope to encompass other states later. Mountain Peak is my present port of call. I anticipate being here several months.'

'Doing what, Reverend?'

'Spreading my Reformed Sinners' Gospel. My lectures and sermons in other towns have converted even hardened criminals to a belief in higher ideals.'

'You mean,' Bart asked slowly, 'that you're aiming to teach the scriptures to the people of Mountain Peak?'

'Well, yes – but I have my own special way of doing it.'

'It'll have to be special, believe me!' Bart grinned. 'I doubt many of the townsfolk are much acquainted with the Bible – though we do have our regular preacher, Harry Levin. He's the local blacksmith, coroner and undertaker as well.'

'Naturally I have no wish to supplant that good gentleman,' Peregrine said affably. 'My own particular lectures and meetings, if I am permitted facilities, will be given on weekday evenings. I intend to prove with my talks that carnal desires are a complete waste of time. The Peregrine Doctrine, you understand.'

Plainly Bart didn't.

'I guess there's no law to stop you speaking, Reverend,' he said. 'No doubt we can arrange for you to borrow our local church . . . But you were asking about accommodation. For yourself, I take it?'

'And for my flock.' Peregrine smiled, glancing towards the shaded window. Bart got up and drew the shade. He gave a start at the sight of some dozen dusty, sweating, and impatient-looking horsemen waiting outside.

'With myself, there are thirteen of us,' Peregrine explained, as Bart wheeled round. 'My converts. Formerly they were tough, lawless criminals, but now they follow me about devotedly, and are an essential part of my tour. Naturally we must all put up somewhere.'

'The only place big enough is the Mountain Hotel, across and a little way down the main street. They'll be glad of the custom, I imagine. Let me know when you are ready to start your lectures, and I'll see if I can help.'

'Most kind of you,' Peregrine murmured, rising. 'Your reward will be a town full of people converted to the Gospel!'

The clergyman left, leaving Bart somewhat puzzled. He watched through the window as the clergyman and his flock went to the hotel across the way – then he left his office and strolled along the boardwalk to the mayor's office, further down the street.

'This is an unexpected pleasure,' Mayor Randle Meredith greeted his son respectfully, rising from his desk.

'I wish you'd remember that you're the mayor and therefore above me.' Bart looked at his father and smiled. 'In the running of this town I take orders from you, remember!'

Randle Meredith differed greatly from his son, both in appearance and aptitude. His surprising grasp of Western technique had earned him the job of mayor. Amiable, loquacious, and never at a loss. Equally brilliant with a .38 and a lariat. Six feet tall, eighteen stone plus in weight, and with the face of a child awakened in the night, he was about the last person one might expect to find in these arid, sleepy wastes.

'What brings you here, son?'

'We've an unexpected visitor – a clergyman. The Reverend Maurice Peregrine, creator of the Reformed Sinners' Gospel and the Peregrine Doctrine. Ever heard of him?'

'Can't say that I have, son. The presence of a Reverend is most extraordinary in this part of the world. Our only visitors as a rule are outlaws!'

Bart gave a shrug. 'Anyway, Dad, my real reason for calling is to inform you that I'm giving facilities to Peregrine to preach his gospel in the church during weekdays. As the mayor you will also have to sanction it.'

'I don't see any problem with that.'

'You might. He has a dozen tough eggs with him,' Bart added. 'He says they're converts, but to me they looked as though they'd kill their grannies for a shoe-lace.'

Meredith smiled urbanely.

'We shouldn't judge any of these visitors until we have seen how they behave. If all is in order, they will be given every help; if otherwise . . .' Meredith's tone gave sufficient explanation.

'Right.' Bart got to his feet. 'Well, I've plenty of paper-work to finish, same as you have, so I'll see you later. We'll ride home for the evening meal and then come back into town. See you at five?'

'Certainly, son.'

Bart returned at the appointed time, when the furious heat of the afternoon was abating. He found Meredith locking his office door on the outside. He turned and adjusted his Homburg comfortably on his semi-bald head. Bart eyed it in some irritation.

'I suppose I'll never convert you to a Stetson, Dad?'

'I'm afraid not. A mark of respect and remembrance to your mother. You know that I wore it at her funeral – and ever since. It must remain.'

'With riding-pants and a check shirt!'

'A useful trade mark, son. I have earned the name of "Homburg", thanks to my hat – just as you have earned the name of "Dude" through your refined Boston accent.'

The two men went down the boardwalk steps to their horses stood at the tie rack. One was Bart's own mare; the other a huge grey stallion, upon which Meredith heaved his bulk. It was one of the few animals in the district that could carry such a load without breaking at the ankles.

Bart gave a backward glance towards the Mountain Hotel as they went.

'I've seen no more of the reverend, Dad,' he said. 'Seems he and his cohorts have bedded themselves down.'

'It all brings business to the town.'

'But what business! Trying to reform the leathernecks of this place with the Gospel! If he'd turned up with a couple of six-guns he'd have stood more chance.'

Not having seen the reverend, Meredith declined to comment. He was still silent when Bart's ranch – the Flying F – was reached.

Jane, Bart's wife, came out on to the porch, her slim hands extended towards him in greeting.

'The days are beginning to drag, Bart,' she said ruefully after he had kissed her. 'Isn't there something I can do in the town, instead of just staying around here like the good housewife? Even that's limited these days, ever since Randle took on Red Eagle and his squaw.'

'You're far from just being that, Jane. And we needed to take Red Eagle and his squaw on to help with the catering for the extra boys in our outfit, now that the Flying F is expanding. Who else but you could run the spread and look after the essentials?'

Jane smiled, letting the subject drop. She was a blonde girl with honey-coloured skin, the result of her outdoor life.

'Be the usual evening meal and then back into town, for both you and Randle?' she asked.

'That's it. A sheriff and mayor have to stay around the town, remember, in case anything happens.'

'But nothing *does* happen these days!' Jane pouted.

'Don't be so sure.' Bart's arm went around his wife's shoulders as they entered the living-room. 'We have strangers in town right now – a reverend and his flock.'

*

The Painted Lady saloon was a surprising place to find a cleric, and yet Peregrine had arrived there at eight o'clock, the height of the evening's business.

Bart and Meredith, standing together at the far end of the bar, surveying the proceedings but not indulging themselves, immediately noticed the small figure in the reversed collar, followed by a swarm of grim-faced men who filed in behind him.

'Good evening, Sheriff,' the cleric smiled, coming over to the bar.

'This is Mayor Meredith,' Bart responded, motioning to his father. 'He is granting you the permission you need to use our church on weekdays.'

'I'm greatly in your debt, Mr Mayor.'

Meredith nodded and beamed, sipping his lemonade. His childlike blue eyes strayed to the tough unshaven gentlemen who were jerking down whiskeys with a startling lack of decorum.

'This is the ideal place to start my campaign,' Peregrine said, gently rubbing his hands and looking about him. 'The harlots and the flesh-pots!'

'I'd suggest, sir, you do not let the ladies and gentlemen present hear you referring to them in that manner,' Meredith advised.

'I only spoke metaphorically, Mr Mayor.'

Meredith shook his head. 'These people don't understand metaphors – only guns, drink, and sex. Primitive, perhaps, but inevitable.'

Peregrine smiled and ordered a soft drink. He looked about him. The air was almost blue with tobacco smoke. The tinny sound of a lone piano was almost drowned by the constant rattle of poker-chips and the buzz of conversation. The habitués of the Painted Lady looked unpromising material for spiritual conversion. The men were cattle-dealers, traders, half-breeds, and simple cowpunchers. The more conservatively dressed women were either their wives or sweethearts, whilst those who were overpainted and underdressed were evidently hostesses working in the saloon.

Suddenly the batwings opened and closed with a vicious swing. Silence fell as eyes fixed on the newcomer, a big, ugly man in black shirt, pants, and hat. A Mexican cheroot dangled from a sensual mouth, and his hairy hands were hovering near the six-shooters at either hip.

' "Hold-up" Hogan, as I live and breathe,' Meredith murmured. 'Extraordinary!'

Bart and the reverend looked at him blankly.

'An outlaw, son. Haven't you yet acquainted yourself with all your reward notices? I found such a circular only yesterday, as I finished sorting the effects of the late mayor. I recognize Hogan from his photograph. He has, apparently, been involved in sundry stage hold-ups and train robberies. There is a reward of one thousand dollars for his capture – alive. So far he has not been indicted for murder.'

By this time "Hold-up" Hogan had reached the bar. His big, florid face had two days of hard iron-grey stubble jutting from it. Cold blue eyes gleamed from a brick-red skin, and a V-shaped scar disfigured one cheek.

'Rye!' he snapped to the barkeep. 'An' quick about it!'

Peregrine's followers glanced at each other significantly, then at the cleric. Evidently they had recognized the outlaw. Peregrine frowned and lowered his empty lemonade glass.

'That man has courage,' he mused. 'Apparently a wanted man – and yet walking calmly into our midst! Promising material for reformation. If a man has courage he is tractable.'

'Not so fast, Reverend,' Bart said. 'I don't want any shooting in this saloon, and we're liable to get it if you try reforming that character.'

'Technically, son, you should place him under arrest,' Meredith remarked.

'Technically, perhaps – but I have only your word for it that he *is* Hogan. Without proof I'm not inclined to interfere at the moment.'

'Are you afraid of him?' Peregrine asked mildly.

'No, Reverend – but I believe in giving everyone an even break. Quite a few cut-throats pass through this town, or hide in it. If they go on their way I don't bother with them. Apparently this man is not a murderer, only a robber of stages and trains.'

'A most roundabout way of saying, son, that you do not wish to try conclusions with Mr Hogan,' Meredith murmured.

Bart shrugged, knowing he could not deceive his father. In Bart there was always a streak of sympathy for the underdog, and at times it made him appear almost a coward.

The cleric stepped forward as Hogan slammed down his empty glass.

'Mr Hogan, I believe?'

'So what?' The outlaw measured Peregrine with his cold blue eyes. 'Take more than a runt like you or anybody else in this dad-blamed set-up to pin me down. I'm hidin' out, see? And this place at the back o' beyond will suit me nicely for the moment!'

'At least you have courage, my friend. I am glad to see that.'

'Who the hell cares what you see? I ain't havin' no truck with a damned parson!' Hogan poured himself another glass of rye and then spat into the sawdust on the floor. 'Beat it, and leave me be.'

Hogan thrust out his big hand suddenly, the palm smacking cleanly into Peregrine's face. He fell back into the sawdust, blinking. The outlaw guffawed and to either side of him the members of the 'flock' tensed but they did not do anything. Though "Hold-up" was not renowned as a killer, he looked as if he could use his six-guns.

Hogan turned back to his drink, then swung round at a tap on his shoulder. He glared at Meredith as he stood beaming at him.

'I'm afraid I must trouble you for an apology to the reverend gentleman. As mayor of this town I am prepared to overlook whatever record you may have and allow you freedom – as long as you stay within the law and do not try to rob anybody – but I must also insist that you treat the citizens with proper respect.'

The outlaw stared blankly, his pale-blue eyes moving up to Meredith's Homburg planted squarely on his head. Then his gaze lowered to the enormous equator, the solitary .38 in its holster.

'You must be Homburg!' Hogan exclaimed abruptly. 'A queer fat guy who wanders around this town with a dude.'

'The dude is the sheriff, sir – and a good one. He's at the end of this bar. Now, concerning that apology—'

'Go chase yourself, fatty! I ain't apologizin' to nobody.'

'Might I then just trouble you to look this way?'

'Huh?' As the outlaw stared blankly Meredith's bunched right fist slammed out with devastating force.

Not expecting the blow, or the tremendous weight behind it, the outlaw reeled back against the counter, slipped, and fell on his back in the sawdust.

'My apologies, sir,' Meredith raised his Homburg momentarily. 'You brought it on yourself.'

'You pot-bellied coyote, I'll—'

Hogan hurled himself on to his feet and then imagined the universe had exploded behind his eyes. He dropped flat on his face, tasting sawdust.

'Just an apology to the reverend, sir,' came Meredith's voice.

As Hogan struggled to his knees, Meredith whirled him on to his feet and suddenly got a grip on his little finger. It seemed a trifling action, but there was a murderous little twitch Meredith could give that finger that made the outlaw yelp with anguish.

'Ju-Jitsu sir,' Meredith explained, beaming. 'Now, that apology, if you please!'

'Hell! My damned finger! OK. *OK*!' Hogan panted. 'I'm sorry, parson! Mebbe I shouldn't have hit you.'

'Perhaps you were just impulsive,' Peregrine murmured.

Meredith released his grip and looked at the outlaw with a snakelike stare.

'As I said, you can stay around this town providing you are law-abiding. Step out of line and either myself or the sheriff will put you under arrest and notify the authorities of your presence.'

The bewildered Hogan seemed about to say something; then he hesitated as the batwings whirled open again and a figure came tumbling in. He ran like a man with the devil at his heels, watched curiously by everyone in the saloon.

'Whiskey!' the man gulped, signalling the barkeep fiercely. 'Before I go loco!'

He drank the spirit at a gulp, then he stood breathing hard, wiping his face with the end of his kerchief.

'What's the matter, Brian?' Bart asked in surprise. He knew Brian Teviotdale well enough – a fairly well-

15

respected citizen and small-time cattle-owner. Usually he was completely imperturbable, but something had obviously scared the pants off him this time.

'Ghosts!' he breathed, licking his lips and glancing anxiously about him. 'That's it! Ghosts!'

The men and women looked at one another. Even "Hold-up" Hogan forgot what he had intended saying and knitted his brows. Bart came forward and gripped Brian by the arm.

'Ghosts!' he repeated. 'Where?'

'Back on the foothills trail. I saw a phantom horseman, Mr Meredith – plain as I see you. It started chasin' me, but I got clear afore he could catch up. 'Nother whiskey!' he finished breathlessly.

Intrigued and interested, the men and women drifted closer, Meredith in the forefront.

'You said "ghosts",' Mr Teviotdale,' he remarked. 'But you referred to a single horseman. Was it one, or several?'

'One.' Brian downed his whiskey. 'It's crazy, Mr Mayor!'

'What happened, exactly?' Bart asked patiently.

'I went over to Skeleton Pass today to get some business done. My way back brought me through the foothills— Then I saw the ghost! Horse and rider white as snow, chasin' me! I rode like hell and just got away. Ain't goin' near those foothills again, *never*!'

'You must have had a spot too much whiskey on the way, Brian.' Bart grinned.

'I tell you I saw a phantom rider! An' I ain't touched a drop till I got in here tonight!' Brian was adamant. 'An' whoever says there ain't such things is crazier than I am!'

Bart glanced at Meredith, who was absently staring into space. "Hold-up" Hogan spat into the sawdust with contempt. The Reverend Peregrine exchanged a look with his flock.

'Some guy musta got killed in the foothills,' Brian went on. 'An' his ghost's come back to haunt the territory. I've heard of such things. My granpaw usta tell me of one over at Plover's Creek, and—'

'Ghosts be damned!' yelled a voice from amidst the assembly, and heads turned to the bearded, middle-aged rancher who was standing on a table. He was evidently fiercely indignant at the story.

'Go and see for yourself,' Brian told him sullenly. 'I don't like bein' called a liar.'

'Sure I'll go,' the rancher retorted, pulling out his .38. 'Any ghost I see'll get lead through his belly mighty quick. Any of you mugs coming?'

'Why go if it doesn't exist?' somebody shouted.

'Yeller, the lot of you,' the rancher growled. 'OK – I'd like to see the phantom that can scare Bob Cook!'

He jumped down from the table and headed purpose-fully through the batwings. Bart looked at his father.

'Oughtn't we to have gone with him, Dad?'

'No reason to, son. If it is a genuine manifestation – which I doubt – it will appear again, and then maybe we can take steps to deal with the phenomenon. Otherwise I fancy we'd be wasting our time.'

Bart nodded. In all conscience, he was glad to escape the task of hunting a phantom in the cold night wind. Then he glanced at Hogan as the outlaw addressed him.

'Where's a place a guy can doss around here, Tin Badge?' he asked. As Bart hesitated, he added: 'Pot Belly said he ain't got objections, remember?'

'Only as long as you stay within the law,' Meredith assented. 'As for lodging, I fancy Ma Doyle's down the street would suit you admirably. You hardly seem to me to be the hotel type.'

17

The outlaw muttered something and then strode off, disappearing beyond the batwing. Reverend Peregrine gave a sigh as the lumbering figure vanished.

'A pity he's gone. I was intending to give him the first lesson in conversion.'

'If you've any sense, Reverend, you'll keep away from him,' Bart snapped. 'I told you so earlier—'

'Sorry, Sheriff, but I don't agree. The harder they are the more readily they break down . . . incidentally, what do you make of this ghost business?'

'Nothing,' Bart answered briefly. 'Trick of the starlight, probably.'

'It wasn't!' Teviotdale snapped. 'I saw a genooine phantom horseman. I reckon Bob Cook'll be singin' a different tune mighty soon – grantin' he survives, that is!'

Perhaps two hours passed in the Painted Lady, time in which Bart and Meredith maintained their apparently idle but attentive guardianship of the townsfolk. From around ten onwards most of the habitués of the saloon began to disperse for home, Teviotdale among them. Then again came the unexpected.

Brian Teviotdale abruptly returned through the batwings in obvious alarm. All remaining eyes swung to him.

'Now what?' Bart asked drily. 'More ghosts?'

'Bob Cook's body is lying just outside of town on the mountain trail!' Teviotdale said, his voice trembling. 'I came on it as I was headin' for my spread. You'd best come and take a look, Sheriff. I couldn't get no movement outa him!'

Bart alerted himself immediately. This was where his office as sheriff was needed. Meredith on one side of him and Teviotdale on the other he left the saloon, followed by several wondering looks. Within seconds Bart and Meredith were in their saddles, following Teviotdale as he led the way out of town.

Once the town was left behind there was nothing but the empty trail, lighted by the glimmering stars. Far away in the distance loomed the darkness that was the mountain range.

'My spread bein' a mile from here I have to come this way,' Brian explained, riding hard. 'We oughta see the body any minute . . .'

He was right. As they rounded a bend in the trail it lay outlined black against the white of the trail itself. Meredith and Bart dropped from their saddles and hurried forward to the motionless figure. Though the starlight was not particularly brilliant, it revealed quite clearly that the man was Bob Cook.

'Dead,' Bart said, feeling for an absent pulse.

Teviotdale was standing nearby, holding the horses. He gave a start as he heard the verdict.

'What killed him? A slug?'

Meredith went over the body carefully, striking a lucifer at intervals. When the last one had expired he shook his head.

'Rather an extraordinary business,' he commented. 'There is apparently no explanation for Mr Cook's death. No sign of a bullet or stab wound, and his throat doesn't bear the marks of strangulation.'

'Heart failure?' Bart suggested.

'In a man as tough as Mr Cook? Unlikely, son. It must have been . . . *something else*!' Meredith looked about him on the silent, starry wastes, out towards the black mountains, and then began an inspection of the dusty trail. Once again his lucifers came into action. Then presently he came back to where the others were standing.

'Strange that there is no sign of Mr Cook's horse, or of any trail belonging to it. In fact, if you examine the dust carefully, you will see that there is no apparent explanation as to how Mr Cook *got* here!'

'But dammit, Dad . . .' Bart broke off, puzzled. 'There must be some markings in the dust showing how he was brought here?'

'There isn't! I think,' Meredith reflected, 'that our best course will be to take this body back into town and have Dr Adey examine it. The cause of death may help us somewhat.'

'It was that blasted phantom that did it!' Brian declared. 'I'll gamble Cook saw the horseman, or it attacked him – and this is the answer. Only a ghost wouldn't leave any prints!'

'The ghost would not,' Meredith admitted, 'but Mr Cook and his horse were both very material and they have not left any prints either! There is nothing else for it but medical examination, and then perhaps another search when daylight comes. I'd suggest, Mr Teviotdale, that you carry on to your ranch.'

'Not sure I like the idea on this lonely trail.'

'We have got past the stage when we like to hold hands,' Meredith commented drily. 'Be on your way, sir, and we will remain here in case you cry out for help. You should reach your ranch within a few minutes from this point.'

Brian nodded in the starlight and swung up to the saddle of his horse. Riding with demoniacal speed, he soon vanished in the darkness. When after few minutes there came no cry or reappearance, Bart turned to his mare.

'Seems he made it OK, Dad. We'd better be on the way with this body.'

'I'll take it aboard my stallion. I fancy the animal will be well able to take the extra load.'

The massive animal did not even budge at the task, and carried both Meredith and the corpse of Cook into town at a steady trot. Dr Adey was at home, though on the point of going to bed. He soon changed his mind when he heard the details, and the body of Cook was carried into the small surgery and laid on the long examination table.

Meredith and Bart stood watching silently in the light of the smoky oil-lamp as the fussy little medico made his examination. At last he straightened up, his face puzzled. 'Death was not caused by gun or knife wound or strangulation, nor can I detect any sign that a diseased heart might have brought sudden death. Only thing I can do is perform an autopsy. The contents of the stomach may explain it – poison perhaps. Or a test of the lungs might reveal something.'

'Could you perform your autopsy immediately, doctor?' Meredith asked gravely. 'This strange death of Mr Cook may be only be the beginning of further trouble.'

Adey nodded and turned to his bag of instruments. He withdrew fluid from the stomach and from a vein, sealing them in phials. Then he performed other tests that the two watching men – Bart at least – did not quite understand. Their next task was to sit and watch whilst the doctor went to work with reagents at his small testing-bench. Dr Adey, in fact, was far more than a medico. In a town as backward as Mountain Peak he ranked as something akin to a magician. A knowledge of science from his training in Denver had made of him an expert chemist and analyst, as well as doctor.

An hour after the body had been brought in he straightened up from his experiments with a look of amazement.

'This man died from sulphuretted hydrogen gas –

absorbed into his blood stream and lungs and stomach in considerable quantities.'

'Isn't that marsh gas?' Bart asked, frowning.

'No, son,' Meredith corrected, thinking deeply. 'Marsh gas is carburetted hydrogen, a very different thing. The sulphuretted variety is one of the deadliest gases known – and how in the world Cook came to encounter it is a mystery. You are quite sure there is no mistake, doctor?'

'None. I'd stake my reputation on it.'

'I must notify the coroner,' Bart said, 'and the legal formalities must be carried out. But the cause of the gas is a complete mystery to me. Unless . . .' Bart shook his head. 'Never mind. We'll leave the body here, Doctor, and Harry Levin – our coroner – can come and examine it. Since Mr Cook had no relatives whom I'm aware of, we are at least spared the unpleasant job of informing them . . . Let's be on our way, Dad.'

Outside the doctor's house both men paused beside their horses.

'I just don't get it,' Bart said. 'It seems to me like a deliberate attack, but who the devil in this region would have the brains to know about sulphuretted gas? All they know around here is the trigger of a gun.'

'The inescapable fact is that somebody killed Mr Cook with that very gas, and it is our job to find out who. I am now much more inclined to believe Mr Teviotdale's story of a ghost than when I first heard it. Right now, however, we are hampered by the darkness, but I would suggest that at sun-up we visit the spot on the trail where we found Cook lying and see if we can pick up any clue. Then there is the matter of his disappearing horse.'

'Perhaps it returned to his home down the main street,' Bart suggested. 'We might do worse than take a look.'

In a matter of minutes they had reached Cook's modest

wooden home at the end of the high street – he had sold his ranch for a fairly prosperous private business – but, though they examined both back and front of the dwelling, the two men failed to discover any sign of the missing horse. The small stable itself was completely empty.

'Do you think it might help matters, son, if we rode out to the foothills in the hope of observing that phantom?'

'Not for me, Dad.' Bart shook his head. 'I've never left Jane alone very late at night, and I don't intend to start now on account of ghosts. Let's just go back home and then investigate in the morning.'

'You go back then, son. There's nothing to prevent me taking a look at the foothills myself.'

'Up to you.' Bart well knew that his father could take care of himself. So when they rode to the front of the building again they went in opposite directions.

In many ways Meredith was ahead of his son. Mysteries intrigued him, and nothing pleased him better than the thought of battle with a clever foe. Twice he had mastered crooks in this particular territory, and here was a fresh challenge. And the use of sulphuretted hydrogen suggested that he was not dealing with a common thug by any means.

Suddenly he became alert. There was somebody coming towards him on the trail, riding at a leisurely pace. Meredith moved his stallion into the ditch and the shadow of overhanging trees, watching as the rider approached.

'Kindly raise your hands, sir,' he ordered, stepping into view, with his .38 levelled.

The horseman reined to a halt and did as ordered. Then, as he went closer, Meredith gave a surprised exclamation.

' "Hold-up" Hogan!'

'Pot Belly! What in hell's the idea of waitin' doggo for me?'

'I'll ask the questions,' Meredith said calmly. 'Kindly dismount.'

Hogan thudded down into the trail dust, keeping his hands up.

'Where have you been, sir?' Meredith asked. 'I need to satisfy myself that you have been acting within the law.'

'You sure are a queer critter,' the outlaw growled. 'I ain't done nothin' wrong. I've been ghost huntin' if you must know!'

'Interesting. What did you discover?'

'Plain nothin' – just like I expected. After hearin' that guy back in the saloon I figured on finding out if he was crazy or not. I guess he was. After I'd booked myself lodging at Ma Doyle's, I rode out here to the foothills. Nary a ghost to be seen.' He spat emphatically into the dust.

'Did you by any chance see a body lying on the trail? Or pass any horsemen whilst on your way?'

'Listen, Pot Belly, I ain't seen bodies, horses or a ghost either. I swears it on my mother's memory.'

Meredith's instincts told him that the uncouth outlaw was speaking the truth.

'Very interesting,' Meredith said. 'Especially as not so very long ago the corpse of Bob Cook was found not so far from here!'

'Yeah?' Hogan frowned. 'Cook? Y'mean that guy who said he was goin' to look for the ghost?'

'The very same. Evidently he found something. Just what isn't clear – all we have is his corpse.'

'Shot?'

'No – he was gassed.'

'That ain't possible, Pot Belly!' The outlaw guffawed. 'Ain't nobody around here likely to know about gas.'

'Someone did. But before you get on your way, a piece of advice: I should not mention to anyone that you have been riding this way tonight. When the people learn of Cook's death they may tie it up with your being in the vicinity.'

'Why the hell should I have killed the critter?' Hogan protested.

'Can you prove that you didn't?' Meredith asked drily, holstering his gun. 'Now get on your way.'

'Very strange,' Meredith murmured to himself, as Hogan remounted and rode off into the night. Then with a shrug he heaved himself back into the saddle of his stallion and continued towards the foothills. He halted at a distance, watching, hoping for something to happen.

Early dawn came – and nothing had happened. Meredith rode back, none the wiser concerning a ghost or the mystery of Bob Cook's death . . .

2

MORE DEATHS

The next day the people of Mountain Peak had learned of the fate of Bob Cook and, the local coroner Harry Levin having returned a verdict of murder by persons unknown, Cook was duly buried during the afternoon in the cemetery at the back of the little church. Finding his killer was up to Bart and Meredith.

A visit to the fatal spot in the daylight revealed no clue as to how Cook's body had got to the place where it had been found. Baffled, they returned to town to consider their next move. They had scarcely returned to Bart's office before the Reverend arrived.

'Did you find anything, gentlemen?' he asked. 'Forgive my asking, but I *am* interested.'

'You and whole confounded town,' Bart growled.

'You know, it may be a real ghost, which would at least account for the lack of footprints . . .'

'Ghosts don't use gas, Reverend,' Bart retorted. 'That poor devil was killed with sulphuretted hydrogen and then dumped on the trail by some mysterious means or other.'

'Mmmm – I had rather overlooked that. Then if we

must have a material explanation, what of that outlaw, Hogan?'

Bart, knowing from Meredith of the presence of Hogan on the trail during the night, tightened his lips and said nothing.

'Though not an avowed killer, he is surely about the most likely one amongst us to have committed this crime. Have you questioned him?'

'So far I have no reason to question him, Reverend. I'm surprised at your suggestion, too. I thought you were going to reform him?'

'Having thought it over, I am not so sure,' Peregrine admitted. 'I have the oddest feeling that the tragedy of last night is somehow connected with him and . . . Anyway, for the sake of everybody's safety, I hope both of you will do your duty.'

With that the cleric smiled, blinked, and then departed. Bart glared at the closed door.

'Is that bright gentleman trying to teach us our business?'

'Apparently so, son – and I don't altogether blame him. I believe the people have had their heads together and elected him to speak for them. In a dilemma, most people look for a handy scapegoat – and that's Hogan.'

'You don't suppose that he—'

'No, son. Cook's death suggests both intelligence and scientific knowledge – neither of them attributes of Mr Hogan.'

Meredith got to his feet and went to the window. As he stood looking across the street a puzzled look came to his moonlike face.

'I take it that the Mountain Hotel provides good meals?'

'What on earth are you talking about, Dad?' Bart joined

27

Meredith at the window. Together they stood watching the members of Peregrine's flock busy loading up the saddle-bags of their horses with provisions from the general stores.

'Odd behaviour for well-fed men,' Meredith commented.

'I'll soon find out what's going on.' Bart yanked open the door and crossed the boardwalk outside.

'Why all the food?' he called across the street. 'Our supplies in this town are not unlimited, remember!'

The men looked at one another uncertainly; then the Reverend Peregrine appeared from the general stores, his arms full of parcels. Bart crossed the street to him and repeated his earlier question and statement.

'I was unaware we might deplete your foodstuffs, Sheriff,' he apologized, blinking. 'I was just taking my flock out for a while, intending to give them an address on the beauty of Nature allied to the Deity. More appropriate to do it in the countryside – hence the food supplies.'

'You've enough to feed an army,' Bart snapped, looking at bulging saddle-bags. 'Surely you aren't afraid these rough-necks will faint by the wayside?'

'Material food is as essential as spiritual,' Peregrine answered, beaming.

'Well, OK,' Bart growled. 'But go easy next time. I have to keep a check on foodstuffs. A remote spot like this has to live on a kind of generous ration.'

Frowning to himself, Bart returned to his office where Meredith stood watching events.

'I take it the Reverend explained himself, son?' he asked.

Bart repeated what Peregrine had told him. 'Not that I believe him,' he added.

'I don't believe it either, son,' Meredith confessed,

fondling his chins. 'There is something peculiar about our clerical friend – and his "flock" even more so. We can't accuse them of anything at the moment, but it will be as well to keep an eye on the gentleman, by following at a distance.'

When the cleric and his men disappeared out of the main street for the north trail to the mountains, the two men hurried outside, mounted their own horses and set off in pursuit.

'I dislike having suspicions of a clergyman, son, but we cannot leave any angle unexamined in this affair,' Meredith said at length.

'I agree,' Bart responded. 'And so far he hasn't done any hot-gospelling, either.'

'On the contrary . . .' Meredith said, drawing rein as they passed the church at the end of the street. Bart followed suit and gazed at a large notice that had evidently been put up outside the church door since the burial of Bob Cook.

DANCE AND SOCIAL TONIGHT!
EVERYONE WELCOME!
AFTERWARDS HEAR THE WONDERFUL
PEREGRINE DOCTRINE
FULL REFRESHMENTS
LOCAL BAND

'Apparently,' Meredith said gravely, 'he's been busy making the arrangements whilst we were out of town looking into the mystery of Bob Cook.'

Both men got on the move again, and after a swift gallop down the trail they came within sight of the Reverend and his flock once more, moving towards the mountains. Keeping at a safe distance – by leaving the main trail and following over the pastureland – Bart and his father never once lost sight of their quarry. Until at last, in open grassland before the actual foothills, a halt was called. Shielded by high hedges, their horses concealed behind the trees, Bart and Meredith lay in the grass watching from a distance.

'Bit late for a picnic and lecture, son,' Meredith murmured, as the saddle-bags were emptied and the contents laid out on a groundsheet on the grass. Bart did not answer. He was busy watching the Reverend giving directions. Then Meredith gave a low chuckle.

'Don't you see what the men are doing? They're preparing the refreshments for the social and dance tonight! Observe the man on the right buttering bread – and his neighbour smearing meat paste or something.'

'Then why the devil couldn't he do it in the town?' Bart got up quickly and strolled down the slope to where the party was busily at work. Meredith followed more slowly.

'Unexpected visit, Sheriff; but none the less welcome.' Peregrine smiled.

'Quite a tea-party you have here, Reverend. When does the address start?'

'Er – I'm afraid it doesn't.' Peregrine sighed, unloading a bag of cakes. 'We've decided to come out here to prepare the refreshments for tonight's social.'

'Why on earth do you have to do things this way? Why didn't you let the general stores handle all the catering?'

'I believe in doing everything for myself, Sheriff,' Peregrine answered. 'It is central to my doctrine to trouble no man. However, I hope you will not spread the information. Some of the guests tonight might not feel too happy about the food if they knew it has been prepared in the open. Flies, bits of grass, and so forth might inadvertently get into things.'

Bart grinned. 'You're an odd cuss, Reverend. All right, I'll say nothing. And that dance-social of yours, followed by an address, seems a good idea. I suppose my wife and I can attend?'

'Of course. I have not had the pleasure of meeting your wife so far. And you, too, Mr Mayor, will be present, I trust?'

'To introduce you to the gathering,' Meredith assented, surveying the foodstuffs. There was a kind of thoughtful wonder in his tone.

'I assume,' the cleric said, after a pause, 'that you followed us out here?'

Bart nodded. 'Your story of a picnic and address did not sound too convincing, Reverend. We have to be suspicious of every odd event whilst investigating the murder of Bob Cook.'

'Surely you do not suppose that I, or my flock, had anything to do with it?'

'Routine investigation includes everybody, I'm afraid,' Bart answered. 'Sorry to bother you, Reverend. See you tonight.'

Meredith gave a final pensive glance round, then followed Brad back up the slope. The ride into town was almost finished before he spoke.

'I cannot understand why any man, unless he be completely crazy, rides three miles into the open country to prepare refreshments for a dance!'

'Peregrine *is* an eccentric, Dad.'

'I cannot think that those thugs with whom he associates would ever consent to being led by an eccentric. I believe the Reverend is extremely wily – but not eccentric.'

'Meaning what?'

'I'm not sure, but something will doubtless develop before long. In the meantime, we'd better return home for the evening meal so Jane can be advised in good time of this affair tonight.'

Eccentric or otherwise, the Reverend Maurice Peregrine certainly did things properly. Bart and Jane – and Meredith – arrived at the church that evening and found that the main ante-room had been completely converted. On the clear floor space the younger girls and boys of the town were dancing to their hearts' content, accompanied by a none-too-efficient band. Around the edge of the floor, on trestles, were long lengths of boarding carrying the refreshments and guarded by the mothers of the town.

At the furthest end of the room a portable pulpit had been erected. Down the front of it streamed a banner proclaiming in silver braid: REFORMED SINNERS' GOSPEL.

'Evidently Peregrine is a better organizer than one would think. See those men over there?' Bart continued, as Jane stood beside him. 'His "flock" – all wearing their best bibs and tuckers, but even now they don't look particularly angelic.'

'I'm wondering,' Meredith murmured, 'what this is all for, son.'

Bart shrugged. 'Presumably to get the folks in the right mood to listen to a speech on conversion. Our friend is perhaps something of a psychologist.' Before the unconvinced Meredith could reply the Reverend Peregrine came toddling up, pink-faced and innocent-looking.

'I'm so glad you've all come. The officials of a town always add dignity to a meeting.'

Bart introduced his wife. Jane smiled and shook hands. 'I'm sure you'll do a lot of good for the town, Reverend. Most of them can do with it.'

'That is why I'm here, Mrs Meredith— Oh, excuse me.

I believe I'm wanted.'

As Peregrine hurried off, Bart and his wife took to the dance floor. Meredith watched them whirling in time with the music, then he retired to a distant chair in a corner to watch the proceedings. He looked asleep, hands locked on his ample middle and eyes half-shut – but he was very much awake. His attention was particularly centred on the Reverend's 'flock', as, one by one, they began to drift away from the gathering by a rear door. When about a dozen of them had disappeared without returning, Meredith got up, and signalled to Bart and the girl that he was going out. He left the ante-room silently and stepped into the cool night wind.

The high street, with its bobbing kerosene-lights, appeared deserted. Apparently everybody in town was attending the dance-social. Though it was anything but a high-class event, it did at least vary the monotony. For several minutes Meredith remained contemplating the lonely vista; then he became alert. There was a sign of activity by the general stores. A buckboard and team was being driven from the side of the stores itself. It swung into the main street and headed out of town, rapidly vanishing in the darkness. Meredith could dimly discern that the buckboard had packing-cases aboard, together with several men guarding them.

Quickly, Meredith went back into the laughter and dancing and sought out Walter Cardish, the owner of the general store. He looked up from a glass of punch as he was tapped on the shoulder.

'Good evenin', Mr Mayor,' he greeted. 'Anything wrong?'

'I think so, Mr Cardish. I believe your store has just been ransacked.'

'Huh?' Cardish nearly dropped his glass. 'Robbed you

33

mean? The hell it has!'

'I suggest I go back with you and make certain.'

Completely sobered, Cardish hurried from the stuffy room with Meredith's enormous figure beside him. Within minutes they were entering the darkened store by the front entrance. Cardish struck a lucifer and lighted the oil-lamp; then he looked about him in dismay at denuded shelves, empty sacks, discarded boxes. . . .

'Who in tarnation *did* this? Did you see them, Mr Mayor?'

'Yes indeed. Can you tell me what you have lost?'

'Looks like all sorts of cereals and tinned foods and tobacco. Enough for a small army! This whole thing must have been planned for when people knew I'd be out!'

'How could they know that?'

'Reckon I told most folk the wife and I were going to the social when they came in to buy stuff. I should ha' kept my mouth shut!'

'Come back to the church with me,' Meredith ordered. 'I may be able to clear this matter up.'

He swung to the door of the store and opened it – then stopped dead as he found himself looking into a levelled six-gun. He recognized the gun-hawk as one of the 'flock' who had stayed behind in the church. He came forward slowly as Meredith stepped back with Cardish behind him.

'Can't keep your fat mug out of anythin', Homburg, can you,' the gun-hawk rapped out. 'I saw you leave with this little guy, so I figured I'd best follow you.'

'Helpfully revealing, my friend,' Meredith murmured, keeping his hands raised. 'But I'll gamble you're not acting alone. The Reverend sent you, did he not?'

'Nobody sent me. When you followed us this afternoon to where we fixed the sandwiches, I figured you was one to

keep an eye on, an' I'm doing it right now. Me an' the boys
don't like bein' spied on, see?'

'Stop fooling around, my friend, and admit it. You're
working for the Reverend, and he's up to something
connected with that so-called ghost which killed Cook.'

'You're crazy,' the gunman retorted, glaring.

'My guess is that you have some more men hidden away
in the mountains and they need food,' Meredith continued implacably. 'This afternoon you tried to get it to them,
the Reverend at the head of things. Then when he realized the sheriff and I were suspicious, some fast work was
done. A dance was arranged, and the food was turned into
"refreshment" to deflect suspicion. I gather you all knew
you were being followed. The dance idea had a second
motive, too. It left the town empty for some of the boys to
make a large haul from here – and at this moment I'll
gamble they're heading towards the mountains with that
loaded buckboard.'

'As smart as you're fat, ain't you,' the gun-hawk said
sourly. 'Well, it ain't goin' to do you much good. You won't
get to tell—'

Out came Meredith's right foot with savage force, and
it cracked on the gunman's shin. Then a huge stomach
butted him in the middle and he went stumbling backwards. Before he had completed his half-fall an uppercut
lashed from somewhere and struck him devastatingly
under the jaw. Dazed, he dropped into a half-open sack of
flour and finished up like a crumpled snowman.

'Get up!' Meredith snapped, pointing his .38 and picking up the gunman's weapon from the floor. 'We are going
back to the church.'

Flour cascading from his clothes, the limping gun-hawk
obeyed. A well-aimed kick sent him outside at top speed.
Thereafter he stood no chance with Meredith and the

furious Cardish behind him. He floundered into the midst of the spectators and dancers in the church ante-room, falling and sliding across the floor like a bearskin rug. Instantly the proceedings came to an abrupt stop.

'What on earth's the idea, Dad?' Bart asked in amazement, seeing the gun in Meredith's hand covering the man scrambling to his feet.

'I fancy the Reverend can explain better than I can,' Meredith responded, and at that the cleric came forward with a puzzled look on his pink face.

'What is happening here, Mr Mayor?'

'To put it bluntly, Reverend, a bunch of your boys have stolen Mr Cardish's grocery stock and dumped it in a buckboard. I saw it happen. Then this oaf came and menaced me with a gun if I dared to say anything. The only person who can explain things is you.'

'Apparently some of my boys have reverted to type,' Peregrine sighed. 'Seeing the town empty, they evidently decided to steal.'

'But why provisions?' Bart asked bluntly. 'Why not the bank?'

Grim-faced, the men and women in the hall moved forward. Peregrine looked about him in bewilderment.

'I cannot be held responsible for what my followers do on their own initiative,' he said. 'When – or if – they return, I'll try and make them see the error of their ways. I'm so sorry, Mr Cardish—'

'Sorry be damned!' Cardish snapped. 'That robbery will cripple me fur money fur months to come! You've gotta put it right! An' what about this critter here who damn near shot the mayor dead? Just goin' to use fancy words to him too?'

Peregrine turned to the sullen gun-hawk. He was knocking flour from his hat and scowling as he listened.

'I figured that as the mayor here was dishing out fancy stories about you, Reverend, he oughta be taken care of,' he growled.

'I'll be frank, sir.' Meredith looked at the cleric as he stood apparently nonplussed. 'I believe you are behind the ghost business in this town, and somehow connected with the death of Bob Cook. I believe the stolen food is to supply some comrades of yours hiding in the mountains.'

The men and women exchanged amazed glances. Peregrine smiled slowly.

'And what exactly are my comrades *doing* in the mountains, Mr Mayor?'

'I intend to find out. I have been suspicious of you all along, Reverend. It's time you came clean.'

'I cannot stop you forming theories.' Peregrine shrugged. 'But you are quite wrong. And I object to you making grave accusations without proof.'

'Afraid he's right, Dad,' Bart said. 'In our official capacity we can't accuse anybody until we have solid evidence.'

'Possibly I have been over-imaginative, Reverend,' Meredith murmured, and gave a moonlike smile. 'My profound apologies. Having a mysteriously unsolved murder in our midst prompted me to jump to conclusions.'

Peregrine shrugged and turned away. He gave the scowling gunman a pitying look, and then went across the open floor to mingle with the assembly.

'What's the idea, Dad?' Bart demanded, as his father holstered his .38. 'Not like you to blunder into saying things without proof.'

'I'm convinced I'm right,' Meredith answered calmly. 'I'd hoped a direct challenge would make the reverend break down, but obviously he is more wily than I thought. I'm satisfied he is the danger in our midst, and that my theory regarding the stolen food is correct. But it may take time to prove everything. Until then I shall be amicable to him.'

'You'd better! The people are beginning to like him – look how well he's mixing with them.'

'What about my stolen stock?' Cardish demanded impatiently.

'I'm afraid there is little we can do at the moment.' Meredith sighed.

'T'hell with that for a story! I'm goin' after them jiggers right now, and I'll blast the daylights outa them . . .'

Before Meredith or Bart could restrain him he swept away across the hall, vanishing through the doorway.

'He's a fool,' Bart growled. 'Anything might happen to him in that mountain area. We're caught up in some kind of intrigue, but I just can't make out what it is.'

'For the moment all we can do is watch – and wait,' Meredith said. 'Sooner or later the Reverend will make a false move, and then we can act.'

'Why wait until then?' Jane asked. 'Why don't we get a posse together and ride out to the mountains? Let's get busy now – and smash trouble before it starts.'

'Unfortunately, Jane, it's not that simple,' Meredith responded. 'Peregrine knows now what we think of him, and will be both vigilant and vindictive on that account. If we went *en masse* to the mountains we would be snuffed out. Just as the unfortunate Mr Cook was – just as, I'm afraid, Mr Cardish will be. We are not dealing with a common cut-throat gunman. As witness the gas method of killing; the mysterious way of returning the corpse. So I repeat – we will watch, and wait.'

Since Meredith usually took the lead in a crisis, Bart and Jane said no more. For the rest of the evening they mingled with the merrymakers, or danced, or sat and talked. They did not dare communicate their fears to Cardish's wife, who spent most of her time anxiously watching for his return.

Then at ten o'clock Peregrine gave his address. It was hard to think, as he talked with fluent conviction of the Gospel, that he might be a villain. Whatever the truth, he had a great majority converted to his way of thinking and promising, before the evening was out, to attend his next address.

Then the assembly began to break up. Bart, Jane, and Meredith stepped out into the cool night air and went over to their horses at the tie rack. Around them, the men and women and girls and boys of the town drifted past, some giggling, some serious, others actually discussing Peregrine's address.

Then came a shock. From a little way down the main street came a cry of horror and a desperate yell for help. Everybody suddenly changed direction and hurried from the church to the point where the sound had originated. Bart moved quickly, followed by Jane, with Meredith lumbering behind.

The scene in the flickering kerosene-light was brutally ugly. A teenage girl was lying in the dust, the angle of her thrown-back head clearly revealing that her neck had been broken. Evidently she had been at the dance, for she was wearing a light and flowery frock, and a fancy ribbon adorned her blonde hair.

Standing over her, half-reeling, held by the vengeful hands of the townsfolk, was "Hold-up" Hogan. He looked bout him with the hunted glare of an animal, licking his lips.

'What's happened here?' Bart snapped, his authority as sheriff enabling him to push his way forward.

One of the women of the town answered him excitedly.

'I was just a-comin' along here from the church, Sheriff, when I saw this no-good critter bendin' over the poor girl here. He's durned well killed her! It's Babs Armstrong,' she added. 'One of the daughters of Joe Armstrong, the livery stable owner.'

'Get this girl to Dr Adey's right away,' Bart ordered. 'She looks dead, but maybe—'

'She *is* dead, son, without doubt,' Meredith commented, rising from testing the pulse. 'Just the same, Dr Adey will need to ascertain the cause of death.'

Silence fell as the girl was lifted into the arms of a nearby cowboy, then it was broken by a cry of horror as her parents came up and realized what had happened. Bart swung round and seized Hogan by the shirt.

'You've plenty to explain, Hogan!' Bart snapped, and with his free hand he took away the outlaw's gun.

'But I tell you I ain't done nothin'!' Hogan growled, rubbing his eyes fiercely. 'I never killed anybody in my life – much less a gal scarce out of the nursery.'

'To hell with that for a tale!' a man yelled. 'You was found pretty near lyin' on top of her!'

'Yeah, sure thing! String the guy up! He's a dirty killer—'

'Wait! *Wait*!' Bart ordered. 'I'm in charge here. What's your version, Hogan?'

'I – I haven't got one,' Hogan whispered. The outlaw swayed a little and seemed to be trying to get a grip on himself. 'I didn't come to the hop, 'cos I'd no decent clothes to go in, an' I guess nobody wants to be friends with a reward-dodger like me. So I went ridin' instead, out towards the foothills, to see again if I could see anythin' of the ghost – I guess I didn't. Things sorta went black. Next thing I knew I was being dragged up and called a killer for lyin' on top of that kid. S'help me, Sheriff, that's all I know.'

'You're not listenin' to those blasted lies are you, Sheriff?' someone yelled.

'How are you feeling now, Hogan?' Bart asked curtly.

'Like a mule kicked me. Why?'

'Come over to the doctor's. I want him to take a look at you . . .'

Suddenly Bart found himself elbowed and shoved on one side, and Hogan was seized by a half-dozen or so grim-faced men. One of them, an elderly rancher, spoke fiercely.

'You're gettin' too soft-hearted t'be sheriff around this town, Mr Meredith! This guy's a girl killer – an' I reckon there ain't no worse crime. We're hangin' the critter right now!'

Bart tried to draw his gun, but before he could level it, the weapon was knocked from his hand by the angry mob.

'Get wise to yourself, Sheriff!' a woman yelled. 'This guy's goin' to get a necktie party . . .'

Helpless, Bart was bumped and shoved to one side whilst the men and women surged past him. Then he found Meredith handing him his gun back.

'They can't get away with this, Dad,' he panted. 'I'm sheriff around here . . .'

'You won't be the first law official who has found it impossible to stem mob hysteria. I'm afraid there is little you can do, son.'

'But you must!' Jane cried hoarsely, shaking Bart's arm. 'If that man's innocent you can't let him die!'

'He's got to have a fair trial anyway,' Bart said, gripping his gun tightly. He hurried forward down the street, with Jane and Meredith right behind him.

The mob had reached the end of the street and was heading for the big cedar-tree with the out-jutting branch upon which more than one law-breaker had met his end.

'Listen to me!' Bart yelled, as he came into their midst. 'Have you gone crazy? This man has got to have a fair trial and—'

'We're satisfied he murdered Babs Armstrong,' snapped a big rancher. 'No trial'd prove anythin' different. Git the rope, Clem.'

Once again Bart was bundled on one side, along with Meredith and Jane. Hogan stood breathing hard, looking helplessly around him in the starlight. Then Meredith recovered himself and stepped forward, his enormous size giving the mob pause.

'You're all going to be pretty ashamed of yourselves if you discover that girl is not dead after all, aren't you,' he said.

'Not dead?' repeated the rancher leading the hanging-party. 'What in hell d'you mean? You said yourself she was dead.'

'Only as near as I could tell – but I am not a doctor. Life may still be there! Somebody go and get the doctor here,' Meredith ordered, and a woman darted off quickly down the main street.

'What's the idea?' Bart murmured, moving up behind Meredith. 'You know as well as I that the girl was finished.'

'A ruse to gain time, son, while I think of a way of extricating Hogan,' Meredith whispered.

Meantime Clem returned with rope. Hogan stood passive and bemused as his wrists were fastened securely behind him; then the remaining length of rope was cast over the tree's lowest branch and noosed.

'Here comes the doc now,' somebody shouted, and in a moment or two the medico come hurrying up and dropped to his knees.

'Well, what's the answer?' demanded the big rancher. 'Is that youngster dead, or ain't she?'

'I'm afraid she is,' Adey responded bitterly. 'Her neck is broken, and death must have been instantaneous – but just the same you can't take the law into your own hands. This man here is entitled to a trial—'

'Like hell he is!'

'String the bastard up!'

Immediately three men seized hold of the free end of rope and the big rancher put the noose about Hogan's neck. He gave a desperate cry – then at the drag on the rope he was yanked backwards. Jane gave a scream of horror and turned away. Bart stood watching helplessly. Then came the unexpected.

Before Hogan could be dragged into the air to the tree-branch there came a sudden earthy thud some yards away from the surging people. They all heard it and turned in surprise. The kerosene-flares clearly revealed the fact that a sprawling body lay a short distance away in the middle of the main street.

3

MOUNTAIN MYSTERY

'What the . . .' Bart gasped amazedly. 'How did that body get there?'

The hold on the rope was relaxed, Hogan remaining with his feet on the earth. As a few men remained to guard him, others hurried forward to where the body was sprawling. Meredith, puffing hard, arrived first. He turned the body over and found himself looking into the dead face of Cardish, the general store owner.

'How in the world did that body arrive?' Jane cried, and gave Bart a helpless look. The entire crowd stared into the dark sky. Nothing but the stars and the silence of the night.

'Release Hogan now!' Meredith commanded, getting to his feet.

'Why should we?' the big rancher argued. 'Just because this body has—'

'Have you no sense?' Meredith shouted, and his sudden anger quelled the murmurings. 'Whoever killed this man here – and Bob Cook – was also responsible for the death of Babs Armstrong. It could not be Hogan who killed this man here, because he was about to be hanged at the time! There is some kind of deadly conspiracy around us, and we have got to hold a council of war. Release Hogan immediately!'

The crowd hesitated, then Meredith's magnetism won the day. Some of the men went back to the hanging-tree and removed the ropes from Hogan. He came forward uncertainly and joined the group standing around the body of Cardish.

'I reckon I owe you, Homburg,' he said thickly, gripping Meredith's arm. 'If you hadn't—'

'I'm trying to dispense justice, Mr Hogan, that's all,' Meredith cut him short. 'Doctor Adey, take a look at this man, will you?' Adey nodded and went down on his knees. He made a brief examination and then got up again.

'Fetch him to my surgery,' he ordered. 'It appears this business is very similar to that of Cook.'

'You too,' Bart instructed, gripping Hogan. The outlaw nodded and accompanied Bart and the surging people down the street to Adey's home. He did his best to keep the great majority of them out, but nevertheless he had to tolerate several people standing around him whilst he made a more thorough examination of Cardish and then a diagnosis of Hogan.

'Well?' Bart asked at last. 'What's the answer, Doc?'

'Cardish died from sulphuretted hydrogen gas, the same as Cook,' Adey answered. 'No sign of knife or gun wounds. Hogan's been chloroformed – earlier in the evening. There are still traces in his respiration.'

'Mebbe that was when it happened,' the outlaw muttered, clenching his hairy fists. 'I was ridin' back to town from the mountains, when I thought I heard somebody ridin' behind me. Before I could look round something' started smotherin' me across the face, and that was when things went black.'

'Obviously you were attacked and drugged,' Bart said grimly. Then he looked about him at the baffled townsfolk. 'Satisfied now? If you had let me have Hogan here examined first, you wouldn't have come within an ace of killing him.'

'Then it was a plant?' somebody asked. 'This critter was purposely dumped on top of Babs to make it look like he killed her?'

'Looks that way,' Bart agreed. 'He was starting to recover when he was found – but even had he still been unconscious he'd have been blamed – and assumed to be drunk.'

'Get the Reverend Peregrine,' Meredith ordered. 'He hasn't been seen since we left the church. Hurry – somebody!' Several people filed out quickly. An uneasy quiet fell on those remaining behind in the surgery.

'What does the law make of it, gentlemen?' Adey asked, looking at Bart and Meredith. 'Why such ruthless murder, and how was Cardish's body returned to town so mysteriously? It fell right out of the sky apparently – yet not with sufficient force to break any bones.'

'Evidently from a low altitude,' Meredith commented, thinking. 'I think—' But before he could speak he was interrupted by a hysterical shriek. The distracted face of Mrs Cardish appeared in the assembly as she pushed her way through to her dead husband.

'I – I've just heard,' she cried despairingly. 'Is he really. . . ?'

'I'm afraid so, madam,' Meredith said quietly, leading her away from the body; then he motioned to the others to try and calm her.

'We've got to take action,' Adey said. 'There is some kind of insidious intrigue at work against this town of ours, and we've got to stop it. How are you getting on solving the mystery of Cook's death, Sheriff?'

'I'm not.' Bart answered. 'But I think answer may lie in those mountains – and I don't mean a ghost, either. That's probably just a scare tactic . . . The one man who may hold the answer is the Reverend Peregrine.'

'Did I hear my name mentioned?' Peregrine himself pushed through the assembly, then he paused and looked blankly at the unmoving bodies of Babs Armstrong and Cardish. He took off his clerical hat, blinked, and looked around him on the hard, menacing faces. 'These good people who came to look for me told me the appalling details. What does it all mean?'

'Quit trying to pull the wool over our eyes, Peregrine!' Bart snapped. 'Two murders in one night! The only ones likely to be responsible are members of your flock – or should I say gang?'

'I don't understand it!' Peregrine said. 'And I resent your accusations. I had nothing whatever to do with these killings, or with the death of Mr Cook. I cannot be answerable for my flock,' Peregrine insisted. 'Possibly they may have reverted to type, but whatever they have done was certainly not under my instructions. Great heavens, man, I am a clerk in holy orders. I preach the Gospel. I believe in the sanctity of life! That you should accuse me of murder, even indirectly, is preposterous!'

The assembly looked at one another uncertainly.

'Where were you when all of this happened?' Bart asked. 'You were not at the attempted hanging of Hogan, nor were you present when the girl was found.'

'I was praying,' Peregrine answered. 'Nothing peculiar in that. I stayed behind at the church after people left to give thanks for the success of my meeting. Then I had to see to the clearing of the room. The church sidesmen who helped me can verify that.'

Bart shrugged. 'We have to take the Reverend's word for it because we can't do anything else. But from here on we have *got* to get action! Cardish died because he went towards the mountains in pursuit of the men who robbed his store. Cook died because he also went towards the mountains. Brian Teviotdale, who first brought news of a phantom horseman, escaped with his life – almost certainly an accident. Lastly, poor Babs Armstrong was killed so blame could be pinned on Hogan. He was only cleared by the return of Cardish's body at a time when he could not have been responsible . . . I'm still convinced that at least some members of your flock are mixed up in it. The mayor here actually saw them robbing Cardish's store tonight, don't forget.'

Peregrine nodded moodily, but remained silent.

Then Meredith asked: 'Where did you first became acquainted with your "flock", Reverend?'

'During my journey to this town I met them on the trail. Feeling somewhat lonely on my trip – and fearing I might be attacked at some point by some desperado or other – I thought it expedient to endeavour to convert the gentlemen to the Gospel. They listened to me as we pitched camp for the night, and I succeeded in converting them to my way of thinking. After which they remained with me, letting me – as I thought – direct them.'

'Interesting,' Meredith mused. 'Then they were already headed toward this town, whether you had come along or not?'

'Perhaps. They merely said they were foot-loose.'

'Why all this talk?' Dr Adey demanded impatiently. 'Where's the point in it?'

'The point, my dear doctor, is that I think we may have been sadly misjudging the Reverend here. He has been fooled into thinking he had converted a gang of ruffians who only remained beside him because he is such an excellent shield for them. Few would suspect the followers of a clergyman as cold-blooded killers and schemers.'

'And also,' Bart said, thinking, 'so all the blame could bounce on to him as their leader.'

'Possibly,' Meredith assented. 'Tell me, Reverend, was preparing refreshments in the fields your idea?'

'No. One of my flock suggested it when there did not seem to be any other place we could prepare the refreshments without giving away exactly what there would be to eat. Keeping an element of surprise in the matter of foodstuffs is half the battle in a little community, I have found.'

'And who paid for the food?' Meredith questioned.

'I did. I keep a fund for such a purpose, made up from donations during my travels.'

'It occurs to me that probably some members of the flock conceived the idea of robbing the grocery store after they'd earlier seen the supplies around them,' Meredith said. 'They were probably trying to smuggle food supplies, at any cost, to comrades in the mountains.'

'Which means,' Bart said, 'that we ought to explore those mountains and bring this business to an end.'

'Exactly so, son.'

'You ought to form a posse of picked men, Sheriff,' Dr Adey said. 'Do the thing properly. I'll volunteer, for one.'

Meredith shook his head before Bart could reply. 'I don't agree. If a whole army of us went exploring the mountains all chance of secrecy would be gone. The less there are of us, the better. As for you, Doctor, you may be needed in town here for an emergency, so that rules you out. The Sheriff and I will take care of the situation between us – as we so often have in the past. Once we have something to go upon we can really act.'

With that Meredith led the way outside and back through the town to where he and Bart and Jane had left their horses.

Jane was looking thoughtful as they rode out of town. 'I know you, Randle!' she said. 'You've got something up your sleeve, haven't you?'

Meredith smiled. 'Perspicacious as ever, my dear. I have indeed. We are not going to find the proof we need in town, but it is possible we may discover something if we can trace where the stolen food has gone. There must be the prints of that heavily-laden buckboard and team.'

'More than probable – but we're riding home, away from town,' Bart said.

'I had thought, son – with your permission – to use the excellent gifts of Red Eagle. Definitely there is no man of our acquaintance better able to do some tracking.' Bart nodded slowly in the gloom, grasping the point. Tracking, to the Navajo Indian, was a natural gift that no white man could ever hope to equal.

The return journey to the Flying F was soon completed. And, when he was aroused and the position outlined to him, the Navajo listened in impassive silence, the blanket he used as a dressing gown wrapped tightly about his lean form.

'Red Eagle find track,' he promised, no trace of expression on his high-cheek-boned face. 'Paleface Meredith will show Red Eagle place where robbery happened. Red Eagle do all he can.'

'Get dressed,' Meredith instructed briefly. 'I'll fix up a horse for you.'

The Navajo nodded and went back into his quarters. In less than five minutes he was ready, in rough trousers and a flannel shirt, a knife sheathed on his belt. He made no comment as he swung to the saddle, but there was nothing unusual about this, for the Navajo had been known to remain silent for days, unless asked a direct question. He was also given to occasional prolonged absences for which he offered no explanation on his return.

The return to town revealed that the townsfolk had evidently retired to bed, for there was not a soul in sight. Opposite the general stores the kerosene-lights had been extinguished. Meredith rode ahead down the main street, pausing at length outside Cardish's store. Bart dropped to the ground, Red Eagle beside him. Immediately, the Indian studied the dust in the dim light, his sight far keener than any white man's. With a thud Meredith slid down from his stallion and came across.

'Large buckboard used by thieves,' Red Eagle said presently, straightening up. 'Red Eagle find hoof-marks of four horses.'

'Can you follow their trail, Red Eagle?'

The Navajo nodded expressionlessly, took the reins of his horse and walked along slowly, studying the ground as he went. Meredith and Bart followed. To them there was only a churned-up area of dust which presently led out of the town and became invisible on the harder ground of the northward trail to the mountains – but evidently Red Eagle could still detect something, for he continued moving until the town itself had been left behind. Then he halted and gazed towards the mountains.

'Trail lead that way,' he said, pointing. 'Maybe to foothills. Do you wish Red Eagle to follow?'

'Definitely,' Meredith answered promptly, then turning to Bart he added: 'I think, son, that it might perhaps be as well if you returned to the ranch. We obviously have an extremely clever enemy and I am thinking of your wife.

Jane is unprotected, and Red Eagle's wife will not be much help. The bunkhouse has its complement of men, I know, but they will all be asleep.'

Transient disappointment at missing out on the action swept Bart's face, but he realized the wisdom of his father's suggestion. He gave a shrug.

'I'll ride back right now,' he assented. 'You'll be safe enough with Red Eagle.'

'I, son, will be safe enough even without Red Eagle,' Meredith answered calmly. With a grin Bart swung to his horse and rode swiftly back through the town. The Navajo returned his attention to the hardly visible trail, noting a stone turned here, a clod of earth uprooted there, and all the time working his way further and further towards the mountain foothills, trailing his horse behind him, Meredith waddling along in the rear with the reins of his stallion in his hand.

How long the tramping and investigating lasted Meredith had no idea, but he was convinced it took the best part of the night, and by the time the foothills were reached he was feeling tired – both from the journey and the sleep he had had to forgo.

'Red Eagle follow trail no further,' the Indian said, pausing, and looking about him. 'No signs on rocks, but horsemen finished journey here. Or else continued through mountains to desert.'

'I think we should look about a little,' Meredith decided. 'If you are prepared?'

The Navajo removed his knife from his belt and the deadly blade glittered for a a moment in the starlight. He looked towards Meredith, his great shoulders and Homburg hat silhouetted against the night sky. 'Red Eagle always prepared.'

They tied their horses to a nearby rock, then as silently

as possible began moving. They kept in the shadow of the spurs to avoid being detected by anybody on a higher altitude who might be on the look-out. However, they had evidently not been careful enough, for a voice suddenly rasped out behind them.

'Don't move another inch or I'll drop yuh!'

At lightning speed Red Eagle swung, flinging his knife at the same time. He was a split second too late, however, for the gunman's .45 flashed sudden flame and with a hoarse gasp the Indian clapped his hands to his forehead, then toppled over on his face. He lay unmoving and there followed the clink of his knife as it fell to the rocks.

'Guess he wasn't so smart, huh?' the gunman asked, coming forward to where Meredith was standing with his hands raised. 'At least you've more sense than to try anything, Big Belly.'

Meredith was peering at the speaker carefully. He thought he recognized him as one of Peregrine's erstwhile followers, but could not be sure in the uncertain light. A gun prodded in his ribs.

'Start movin', Mr Mayor. The rest of the boys will want to talk to you.'

Meredith obeyed and the way he was forced to go took him high up into the foothills amongst rutted trails and rocky defiles. His captor kept close behind him, his gun ready for immediate action. Meredith's thoughts went back to Red Eagle. He had no idea whether the Indian was dead or only badly wounded.

As he climbed higher Meredith realized that he might be walking straight to his death. When other gunmen joined this one – who had evidently been acting as look-out – there would be no chance of escape.

Suddenly Meredith swung round violently. The other man, right on top of him, was not expecting it and received that gigantic stomach straight into his own with battering-ram impact. He gulped a little and then, to his utter amazement, a terrific left hook to the jaw knocked him flat on his back, his gun flying out of his hand.

'My apologies,' Meredith murmured, snatching back his own gun from where the gunman had slipped it in his belt. 'Now it's your turn to do as you're told. Get on your feet.'

Swearing luridly, the man obeyed, his hands spread wide as though poised to fling himself on Meredith – but he had the good sense not to. Meredith moved slowly forward and pulled his remaining gun from its holster, flinging it out over the cliff edge at the side of the mountain trail. The remaining gun he kicked after it. Weaponless, the man waited, breathing hard, his hands raised.

'Now, my friend, you will provide me with some information,' Meredith continued. 'It concerns the provisions stolen tonight from the town's general stores.'

The man did not answer. Meredith gave him a few seconds, then slashed the back of his hand across the man's face. He gave a gasp of pain.

'You dirty, fat coyote! I'll kill yuh for this! I'll—'

The man broke off again with a yelp as for the second time Meredith's hand swung across his face, this time in the opposite direction. Infuriated, he forgot all about the gun and lashed out with his fist. It was a lucky blow, and Meredith staggered backwards, taken unawares. A second blow under the jaw knocked him from his heels as he tried to recover himself – then his feet went from under him and he was falling heavily down the face of the cliff at the side of the trail.

Meredith clutched frantically as he slithered and dropped. Unexpectedly his fingers suddenly gripped a jutting spur and he clung on to it desperately, wondering if it would take his huge weight. It continued to hold as he swung to and fro. Up above, his assailant peered down into the depths, but the starlight was too dim for him to see anything, and in any case Meredith was below the rock with only his hands visible. The man turned away with the conviction that Meredith had plunged the full 300 feet to his death.

The drop below was almost sheer and Meredith realized he had only a few minutes at most to save himself before his grip slipped. He made the only move he could – to try somehow to climb on to the top of the rock spur whilst he thought out what to do next. Cursing his enormous girth he began struggling and heaving. Even so there was muscle enough below the fat, and after considerable effort he had managed to scissor his fat legs round the jutting rock and crawl his way up until he was on top of it. Astride and triumphant he mopped his face with his kerchief and felt for a Homburg hat which was no longer there.

When he had recovered sufficiently he gazed above him – to where the stars were beginning to pale before the dawn. It seemed a long way to the top of the cliff – and an even more preposterous distance to the bottom of it. He was trapped.

His despairing thoughts were abruptly cut short as something like a snake whizzed close to his face and then began to swing back and forth. It was a second or two before, in the uncertain light, he realized that the thing was a rope.

Meredith hesitated. At the other end of the rope there might quite easily be his assailant, or some other gunman. He angled his head up cautiously. Against the brightening sky he could distinguish broad shoulders and a head, with lank hair falling to either side. Obviously Red Eagle, though the why and wherefore of his escape from the bullet in the head remained a mystery.

He hesitated no longer. Gripping the rope he started to haul himself upwards – then he found that his immense weight was being hauled for him. He dug his feet into the cliff face and went up horizontally, staggering at last over the edge of the escarpment and casting away the lariat tied to the horse that was dragging him.

The Indian came forward, the silk square he usually used as a handkerchief now tied about his forehead. He tapped it as Meredith studied it.

'Bullet only glance,' he said. 'Red Eagle soon recover and look for you. Follow trail to here. Another trail goes back into foothills.'

As he dusted himself down, Meredith tersely explained what had happened to him. As the Navajo remained silent, Meredith asked: 'What about our horses? You have this one, but where is my stallion?'

'Where you leave him. I not bring two.'

Meredith wasted no further time. He was worried lest at any moment a shot would come whanging down which would finish him and the Indian. But nothing happened. They escaped from their exposed position, Red Eagle riding his horse and Meredith slithering and stumbling down the rocky defiles until at last he reached his stallion. The half-sleeping beast awoke instantly as eighteen stone plus landed in his saddle, then, glad of the chance for activity, it began moving swiftly, Red Eagle riding hard in the rear.

By the time the Flying F had been reached the sun was fully up and Bart was in the yard saddling his horse. He stopped as the two came riding in.

'I was about to set out to look for you,' he explained,

coming over. 'What happened?'

'Quite a deal, son.' Meredith dismounted and breathed heavily. 'I suppose I'm too late for breakfast?'

'We've had breakfast – but both of you look all in. Jane and I will fix you up.'

Meredith followed his son into the ranch house, still feeling for his missing Homburg. Then to his surprise he felt something jabbing him in the back. It was the hat, in the hand of the Navajo.

'Red Eagle find this at place where you fall,' he explained. 'Red Eagle put it in saddle-bag of my horse.'

'My eternal thanks,' Meredith murmured, looking and feeling a new man.

Once within the ranch house he washed and changed, and by the time he had done this a man-sized breakfast of ham-rashers and fried eggs was waiting for him.

'Eat,' Bart ordered. 'Jane – coffee for Dad.'

With a smile Jane poured it. Red Eagle, at the other side of the table, maintained his usual stoic silence, but presently Meredith started explaining – and by the time he had finished the meal was over.

Meredith sat back from his plate contentedly and dabbed at his lips with the napkin.

'Have I your permission to smoke, Jane, whilst I state a few theories?'

At Jane's nod, Meredith rolled himself a cigarette with astonishing deftness, one-handedly, and stuck it between his cushiony lips. Red Eagle got to his feet.

'Red Eagle go to wife. Wife put Red Eagle's head in order. It ache,' he said,

'I'm not surprised,' Jane murmured. 'Nobody but a Navajo would have survived a wallop like that and then ridden home to breakfast . . .'

'Just a moment, Red Eagle,' Meredith said, and the

Indian halted on his way to the door. 'As soon as you've got your wound fixed, I'd like you to rejoin us in here. I've a few questions for you.'

Red Eagle merely grunted and went out.

His cigarette drawing to his satisfaction, Meredith sat back in his chair and mused for a moment, a faraway look in his baby-blue eyes.

'Whilst Red Eagle and I didn't penetrate as far into the mountains as I'd intended, doesn't it strike you as odd, son, that we only encountered a single lookout?' he said presently.

'Yes, that thought had occurred to me.' Bart frowned. 'We know that about a dozen of Peregrine's flock defected and decamped to the mountains . . .'

'And there are probably others there too,' Jane put in. 'The amount of provisions they stole suggests that.'

'Then where were they?' Bart mused. 'Not to mention their horses.'

'The fact that Red Eagle was able to rescue me, and that neither of us was attacked again, leads me to think that the main party of men and horses was not on the mountain – but *inside* it! That would account for them not observing us, or coming after us. The look-out we encountered thought we were dead, and had probably moved to a new location, or possibly he went to report.'

'You mean into a cave – or series of caves?' Bart said.

'Possible, but there's another explanation, which I want to check with Red Eagle.'

'And where does Peregrine tie up with it all?' Jane asked, mystified. 'It doesn't begin to make sense to me.'

Meredith got to his feet slowly, and stubbed out his cigarette in the brass ash-tray. 'I have a theory, Jane – son,' he said, musing. 'But I prefer to wait until Red Eagle is here before discussing it.'

After several minutes had elapsed, Meredith turned impatiently in his chair and rang the bell that was used to summon Red Eagle from the domestic regions. The Navajo came in silently and looked from one to the other with his implacable dark eyes.

'We need to have our talk, Red Eagle,' Meredith explained. 'Tell me, as a Navajo, are you well acquainted with the mountain district?'

'Red Eagle know all territory for twenty miles around Mountain Peak Valley,' he replied, without a flicker of interest.

'That being so, do you know of any particular Navajo tunnels or catacombs in the mountain region, big enough to hide a large party of men and horses?'

The Navajo remained silent for a moment or two, his high-cheek-boned face looking as though it were carved out of teak: then he seemed to remember something. 'There are the Halls of Manuza,' he said finally.

'Who the devil's Manuza?' Bart asked, astonished.

Meredith coughed primly. 'Hmmm, I have – as the saying is – "swotted up" on Navajo history since Red Eagle joined our service, and I believe Manuza was one of the ancient Navajo tribal leaders, and a remarkably popular individual in his day. Much hunting, much riches, if you grasp my meaning.'

'Red Eagle descended from the race of Manuza,' the Indian said, with noticeable pride, and he raised his square chin. Meredith asked another question.

'Would the Halls of Manuza be a series of very big tunnels – or even one big tunnel – that might be entered from an opening in the cliff face?'

The Navajo merely nodded.

'At the limit of the northward trail?' Meredith persisted. 'Beyond the spot where we fought last night?'

'Yes, Paleface Meredith. But the entrance to the halls has been blocked by my ancestors after the white men came to our land. There is another door to the south, in Lone Mountain, but it is only known to my people . . .' The Navajo broke off, and scowled. 'Red Eagle not want to talk further.'

Bart exchanged a surprised glance with his father. Meredith was looking decidedly complacent.

'Lone Mountain, son, as I hardly need to tell you is that solitary peak to the south which, by a chain of low hills eventually passes round the back of the valley and joins the main mountain group.' Meredith sat forward a little. 'When you say there is a door to the north and the south, do you mean there is an underground connection?'

'The Halls of Manuza. Red Eagle not say more.'

Meredith ignored the implication and continued relentlessly: 'Are there any treasures left, Red Eagle, or has your race removed them all?' The Navajo did not reply, and from the hard set of his face it was plain he did not intend to.

'All right,' Meredith said, beaming. 'Maybe that was not a fair question. Thanks for the information you've given.'

'Red Eagle ask question,' the Navajo said. 'Is Paleface Meredith attempting to penetrate the Halls of Manuza?'

Meredith shook his head. 'I am not, Red Eagle, but the man who calls himself the Reverend Peregrine is. At least I think so. There is evidence – admittedly circumstantial as yet – that points to it.'

'He will die with my ancestors,' the Navajo muttered, his sinewy hand dropping to the knife he had evidently recovered. 'I find Paleface Peregrine and kill—'

'Hold it!' Bart jumped to his feet and caught at the Navajo's arm as he made to leave the room. 'You can't go dashing off killing people! You're supposed to be civilized

– more or less.' Red Eagle looked at him with burning eyes.

'If this paleface enter the halls of my ancestors, I kill. That is the law. Not I alone, but many others. I can call them together.'

'Well, don't do it just yet,' Bart implored. 'There's something very queer going on, and the desecration of your ancestors isn't the only thing. We're trying to sort it out – and we will. On your oath, you are not to do anything until you have permission.'

Red Eagle considered for a while, then his hand dropped slowly from the hilt of his knife. 'Red Eagle obey – for a time,' he answered ambiguously, and went out.

Troubled, Bart returned to the table where Meredith and Jane were both looking at him. 'Once let an Indian get a revenge complex and anything can happen. If he kills Peregrine without any apparent reason, we'll be held responsible by the authorities since he's under our control.'

'Right now, son, I venture to think we can forget him for the moment,' Meredith commented, struggling to his feet. 'We have made the interesting discovery that Mountain Peak – or at least the surrounding mountains – contain hitherto unsuspected catacombs. Whether our friend Peregrine is trying to steal hidden treasures or is aiming at something else we don't yet know.'

'There's something that doesn't quite hang together,' Jane said. 'Red Eagle said the north entrance tunnel was blocked, and that only he – or his fellows – knows where the southern entrance is, so—'

'But that is just the point, madam,' Meredith said, beaming. 'Obviously, the men in the mountains, having discovered the north entrance, are busily engaged in *unblocking* it. They are unaware of the other entrance.'

'I think you've got something, Dad!' Bart exclaimed, his eyes bright. 'If the Navajos made a thorough job of blocking the tunnel – as presumably they did – it would take an entire small army of men to shift the barrier . . .'

'And that,' Meredith said, 'is exactly what I think they are doing. And making good progress, apparently, since they have already disappeared into the tunnel itself.'

'And the ghost rider and murders?' Bart asked. 'Where do they fit in?'

'We don't yet know, son, but it's possible that they are some kind of scare tactic to deter anyone from going near the mountains whilst their excavations are proceeding.'

'And they've certainly succeeded so far,' Jane gave a little shudder. 'After what's happened the townsfolk are giving the mountains a wide berth.'

'*They* may be doing so, but we are not so circumscribed,' Meredith said, getting to his feet.

4

NIGHT ATTACK

Ten o'clock the following morning found Bart and Meredith on their way along the mountain trail from Mountain Peak, carrying with them enough provisions for two days and a full supply of ammunition. They rode in the morning sunlight, alert for anything unusual, leaving behind them a much-disgruntled Jane, who had begged to be included in the expedition – and had been refused. Bart was not prepared to take the risk of her becoming involved in what might prove to be a gun battle. Red Eagle had been instructed to remain at the ranch as additional protection for Jane should anything be attempted there in their absence. By this time both he and Meredith knew the ruthlessness of the menace they were fighting.

'It is to be hoped, son,' Meredith remarked, a mile along the trail, 'that we discover something, otherwise the populace is liable to become restive. Three unsolved murders have set them on edge.'

'We'll do our best,' Bart growled. 'But what baffles me is how did the body of Cardish drop from nowhere, and if the Reverend isn't behind things, who is?'

'We can only hope to precipitate events that may reveal some clue. As to the body that fell from nowhere . . . there *is* one possibility that occurs to me, but I can't think it very likely out here in Mountain Peak. The only explanation that readily suggests itself is from a balloon.'

'Couldn't have been that. A large, slow-moving object like that would have been seen. From all accounts the body only fell a short distance, and even if we didn't see a balloon in the night sky we'd have heard its burner as it passed over us. There wasn't a sound. I remember that distinctly. And besides, people in this region don't use any such contrivances.'

'People who will use sulphuretted hydrogen for killing purposes, and chloroform for drugging, might be capable of other scientific tricks,' Meredith pointed out. 'We are not dealing with hill-billies in this business but somebody extremely ingenious.'

Meredith straightened his Homburg and surveyed the pasturelands and the sweeping fields of golden brittle bush stretching away almost to the foothills. He found it possible to enjoy its beauty in spite of the gravity of their mission. Bart had no such power of detachment. His thoughts centred solely on three murders and what lay behind the crimes.

Within a mile of the foothills, Meredith halted his stallion for a moment and looked about him.

'Apparently, son, we've not yet been observed – or else it is not good policy to attack us in the daylight. I would suggest that if we leave the normal trail and make for that higher level there' – he indicated an ancient arroyo winding down from foothills – 'we might find a vantage point from where we can survey. We'll snatch a meal and then explore further on foot.'

Bart nodded and urged his mare forward again. The

ascent of the arroyo revealed a clearing surrounded with massive rocks. The blazing noon sun poured down on both men as they dismounted and looked about them.

'We can command an excellent view from this base,' Meredith said. 'But first we had better get ourselves and the horses into the shade and have a meal.'

As they ate, the two men surveyed the mighty ramparts above, and then the slopes below. Bart frowned as he rested his back against the rocks. 'Why all this elaborate ghost business and the murders? Perhaps the ghost is intended to frighten casual prowlers away from these mountains, and the mysterious murders to keep people in their homes?'

'Sunlight, son, would probably reveal the "ghost" for the fake it is. That, I fancy, is the explanation for our present immunity. Finish up your meal, and we'll investigate further.'

They spent the afternoon crawling in and out of the rocks, surveying from all reasonable vantage points without making themselves obvious to a look-out – but as far as they could tell the region they were in was deserted. Bart's disappointment was palpable as they returned to camp in the evening light, but Meredith did not seem greatly disturbed as he began to arrange a second meal.

'These foothills cover a tremendous area. To explore them satisfactorily we'd have to constantly change our base. I suggest we remain here well into the night and see if any ghost rider appears. If one does not, then we shall have to consider returning home for more supplies to sustain us for a longer search. Those men who stole the provisions must be in these mountains somewhere. They didn't return to town, remember.'

'Pity we can't pick up the tracks of their buckboard,' Bart growled, looking down on the normal trail that led through the foothills to the other side of the range.

'Impossible, son, I'm afraid. The wind through this pass keeps dust constantly on the move. Unless the track is very new it is impossible to find it. Dust covers it over. Red Eagle did well to trace it as far as he did last night, but that was when the trail was new.'

Thereafter, as the sun crept down the sky and became a blaze of silver and vermilion behind the mountain peaks, they finished their meal and drank water from their canteens.

'I suppose they'll have buried that poor devil Cardish and the Armstrong girl by now,' Bart remarked, gazing out into the purple haze to where Mountain Peak was dimly visible against the vast pasturelands. 'Your about-face concerning Peregrine surprised me, Dad.'

'Yes, I now think he's an innocent party – for the reasons I gave last night. He is, I believe, simply being used by the thugs as a shield. But that, unhappily, does not bring us any nearer the identity of the *real* culprit.'

'Who may not even be in Mountain Peak at all.'

Silence again, and the sun crept lower. In the distance the white trail which led through the darkness of the fields began to disappear as mist crept across it – until Bart suddenly gave a start and pointed.

'Am I crazy, Dad, or is there a rider out there? A real one?'

Meredith looked intently at the distant, slowly growing speck as it came towards them. He wheezed to his feet and dug the field glasses out of the equipment.

'It's your wife, son,' he exclaimed, handing the glasses over.

'Jane? Can't be!' But the lenses satisfied him that Meredith was right. The distant speck leapt into relief as a woman in white blouse, leather sleeveless jacket, and black riding-pants, an orange kerchief blowing in the wind about her throat. She was riding hard and steadily in the direction of the mountains.

'We'd better signal her,' Bart said quickly. 'If she continues following the main trail down there she'll miss us completely . . . but when we signal we may give ourselves away,' he added irritably, lowering the glasses. 'Why the devil didn't she stay at home?'

Before Jane's distant figure had come clearly into view night fell with the abruptness of a drawn blind. The stars glittered vividly out of the purple sky, and a chill wind stirred. Far away the kerosene-lights of the town began to dance like fireflies.

'I'll go down to the trail and stop her as she comes past,' Bart said, handing the glasses back and going over to his mare. 'You stay here, Dad, since we'll be using this base for tonight at least.'

'OK, son. I— Look!' Meredith broke off. 'A ghost rider!'

The two men stood gazing in fascination at the trail that ran below this lofty vantage point. From the far distance a white, elusive speck was approaching, growing gradually larger and moving swiftly.

'Jane must have been seen approaching, and now night's come the ghost can get busy,' Bart said, drawing his gun. 'We probably missed being spotted because we branched away from the main trail . . . I'm going after that damned ghost and get Jane at the same time.'

Quickly he coaxed his mare forward and down the slope of the arroyo, the animal slipping and sliding for a good foothold.

The sound of beating hoofs was coming from two directions at once, from left and right. Obviously Jane was speeding along, and so was the 'ghost'. One thing was at least being proved: that the horse, white as its rider, was no ghost. It made far too much noise for that.

Then Jane came into Bart's view as a dim figure in the starlight, outlined against the white of the trail. She saw the ghost rider hurtling towards her at that moment and dragged her horse to a slithering halt. Then she swung round and began to ride back whence she had come.

'Jane!' Bart yelled hoarsely. 'Jane, come back here . . .'

She was too far away to hear him. He swung round to look at the ghost rider, and at the same moment a shot exploded from it, sending a bullet whizzing close by his head. Evidently the 'phantom' had heard his shouts and was trying to pin his position. Bart fired back at the bobbing, glowing rider and his mount as they still came on. Whether or not he had scored a hit, the apparition dragged to a halt and then began travelling in the opposite direction.

'Leave him to me, son,' Meredith shouted, and Bart glanced up in the gloom to see the stallion plunging clumsily down towards the trail. 'You look after your wife.'

Bart swung promptly and dug in the spurs, hurtling his mount along the trail in the direction Jane had taken. Even so it was some time before he caught up with her in the starlight, and it was only because he had shouted. It dawned on him as he drew level that she had mistaken the drumming of his horse's hoofs for those of the ghost rider.

'Bart!' she gasped thankfully, as the two beasts came to a halt side by side and he put an arm about her shoulders. 'I – I thought—'

'That the ghost was chasing you? Dad's chasing him right now, and I think I may have winged him.' Bart paused to let her catch her breath, then added: 'What on earth brings you here?'

'I came to warn you that Red Eagle and his wife have

left the ranch. I discovered that they'd slipped away a few hours after you'd left. I thought he might have been coming to attack you for invading his sacred tunnels, or something.'

'We haven't seen him – and he'd hardly be likely to bring his wife along with him if he planned on attacking us would he?' Bart commented. 'Besides, you could have asked our foreman or one of the boys to come after us.'

'Well, yes – but to be frank I couldn't bear the thought of being left out of things. Besides, when I knew it would not be long before darkness came I didn't like the idea of being on my own in the ranch – so I came out to find you.'

'But the Flying F boys would be in the bunkhouse. You'd be safe enough.'

'I know, but— Well, I came anyway.' Jane's voice was defiant. 'I calculated that you'd see me or I'd see you before it got dark, but I was a bit out in my reckonings.'

'OK, sweetheart,' he murmured. 'Better come along back to the base camp we've got in the foothills.'

They began riding back the way they had come, prepared as they went for sudden and unheralded attack. They reached the arroyo in safety and went up it to the enclosure in the rocks. Wearily, Jane dropped from the saddle of her pinto and drew her leather jacket more tightly about her.

'Here, try this.' Bart handed her a blanket. 'You ought to have known the mountain air's mighty cold at night.'

'I didn't think. It was blazing hot when I left the spread . . .' Jane draped the blanket about her and settled down amidst the rocks.

They both tensed at the sound of approaching hoof-beats. A horseman became visible on the trail; it proved to be Meredith.

Presently he had brought his stallion up the arroyo and

tied it with the other two animals. It looked oddly as though his right forearm and hand was crawling with light as he moved. Then the light dropped to the dust and remained there, glowing.

'Part of the "phantom",' Meredith explained. 'Canvas, covered in phosphorescent paint. I pursued him for about a mile, during the course of which he emptied his revolver at me – but missed in the dim light. Then, having no more ammunition, he tried to escape by sheer speed. I couldn't shoot at him because I wished to question him, so I threw a lasso. I missed, and the noose settled on his saddle horn. My sudden pull on it ripped away this piece of canvas. Our ghostly friend got away – but I would remark that he left bloodstains in the dust of the trail!'

'So I did wing him!' Bart exclaimed. 'That's something, anyway.'

'Good evening, Miss Jane.' Meredith inclined his Homburg-hatted head towards her. 'Enjoy your ride?' he added drily.

'I'm fine, Randle – and thankful that Bart found me.'

Bart picked up the piece of phosphorescent canvas and examined it carefully. Everywhere his hands touched they picked up the softly glowing paint.

'Presumably the horseman and the animal itself were covered in canvas treated with this stuff.'

'Simple, but effective enough to scare a lot of back-woods inhabitants, son – as witness the alarm of Mr Teviotdale when he first saw the apparition.'

'You've proved the phantom is a fake, anyway,' Jane said. 'So what happens next?'

'I thought we might follow the trail of our departed ghostly friend,' Bart remarked. 'It will be dangerous, but it has to be done. Jane, you'll have to stay here, and – *take cover!*'

He broke off and suddenly hurtled himself to the shelter of the rocks, dragging Jane with him as the night was split by a rattling staccato of bullets. They came from overhead in a murderous hail.

Meredith, too, stumbled into safety as fast as bulk allowed, but he paused long enough to kick the glowing phosphorescent chunk of canvas over the edge of the clearing and down to the trail.

'May be acting as a marker, son,' he panted, blundering forward. 'If so—'

'Look up there!' Jane cried abruptly.

The gunfire had ceased now. Bart and Meredith were staring intently upwards as, against the brilliant stars, a weird shape swept overhead. It looked like a monstrous moth with extra wings, moving soundlessly into the distance.

'That's where the firing came from,' Bart said. 'We're safe for the moment.' As they emerged from their hiding-place, Bart added: 'But what the hell was it?'

They watched the dark shape becoming smaller against the stars until it faded in remoteness.

'Looked like something prehistoric,' Bart commented.

'Firing shots at us? Hardly prehistoric, son,' Meredith responded drily. 'That object was, I think, a glider of very modern design, and painted dead black so it is not visible in the darkness. To launch it from the mountain heights would be simple.'

'A glider!' Bart exclaimed. 'What the hell's a "glider"? I never heard of it. Is it some kind of flying-machine?'

'A quite modern development, son – but the idea of a heavier-than-air flying-machine is not exactly new,' Meredith murmured. 'As long ago as 1804 an English experimenter, Sir George Cayley, built a small model glider, a rather flimsy affair but astonishingly modern-looking. He continued to experiment, and actually built a crude hot-air engine, which – had it been successful – might have achieved the dream of powered flight when fitted to a glider. He suggested biplanes might be suitable as a means of obtaining the maximum lift for the minimum of weight of structure. Cayley even experimented with full-size gliders, in one of which a young boy and, perhaps, his coachman, are said to have made short flights.'

Meredith beamed as Bart and Jane looked at him, open-mouthed. His erudition on out-of-the-way matters always surprised them.

'Other experimenters have carried on his pioneering work, and tonight we evidently witnessed a modern version. The idea actually occurred to me when the bodies of Cook and Cardish reappeared so oddly, only I could not quite believe that such a modern device was being used out here in the West. Now I know my guess was right . . . We are dealing with people who use a glider, sulphuretted hydrogen gas, and chloroform. Quite modern, son, quite modern.'

'Obviously,' Jane said, musing, 'the base of operations cannot be far away. Our wounded phantom friend must have got back home and told what happened to him. The glider was launched and an attack made on us as it swept past. Probably the ghost rider said we might have a chunk of illuminated canvas marking our position.'

'Excellent deduction, Jane!' Meredith murmured approvingly. 'But I think we might be unwise to try and find it in our present negligible strength.'

'But I thought you said the more of us there were the less chance we stood,' Bart remarked.

'That was before we had any conception of where the base of operations lay. Now we have a reasonable idea I think it would be best to return to town, organize a posse, and attack in strength. It is just possible that our murderous friend in the glider believes he has disposed of us.'

'That glider must have come to earth somewhere,' Jane pointed out. 'Shouldn't we try looking for it?'

Meredith shook his head. 'Too risky. I imagine that at night many look-outs are on the watch – as witness the fates of Cook and Cardish . . . Our best course is to return home by the widest detour possible.'

Together they collected up the various pieces of camping equipment lying around. This done, the horses were mounted and the trio began the difficult descent to the trail. Aided by the darkness, they detoured some five miles round the back of the range, moving through passes and clefts before striking out for the main trail leading back to Mountain Peak.

'This glider business fascinates me, son,' Meredith commented, as they rode along. 'A glider relies on a particular wind current for its successful launching, and these mountain heights are an ideal spot from which to launch it. At night the wind is favourable for a glider journey from these mountains to the town below. In daylight the wind is in the opposite direction, which has probably something to do with lack of action by day. Not that our ingenious friends would take the chance of revealing their glider in daylight in any case.'

'When we attack in force we'll need a good strategy, otherwise most of us are likely to be picked off like clay pigeons,' Bart remarked. 'But why are these ingenious people in this region at all? What are they after?'

As no one knew the answers the conversation lapsed until, eventually, the Flying F was reached.

The ranch was dark and apparently deserted, the lights being out in the bunkhouse. But evidently Kevin Briggs, their foreman, was on the alert awaiting their return. He emerged with ready guns to check up on the sounds as the trio rode into the yard. Satisfied, he returned to his quarters.

The three took time enough to have a brief supper and then went to bed. But if they had imagined they had made their entire trip unnoticed they were mistaken. Some little distance from the ranch four horsemen were hidden in the shadow of the trees, their attention fixed on the spread.

'Give 'em time to settle down in their beds, then we'll act,' the leader murmured. 'Got those gas bombs OK?'

'Uh-huh,' another whispered. 'More'n enough.'

'OK. We'll tackle the bunkhouse first, an' any dogs there may be lurkin' around. Tie our horses to these trees, an' we'll move in on foot.'

The four dismounted, secured the animals, and then glided in the direction of the ranch. Kevin Briggs, now that his employers had returned, saw little reason to maintain his exacting vigil, and was half-asleep at his post near the bunkhouse doorway, waiting to be relieved. Certainly he was too bemused to notice the shadowy quartet gliding across the yard. He only became aware of the attack when a forearm clamped under his chin and he was dragged backwards. He struggled briefly and then sagged helplessly as the butt of a gun slammed down on the side of his head.

'OK, hurry it up with the gas bombs,' the leader murmured.

One of the men dug his hand in the satchel he was carrying and threw two small bombs into the midst of the bunkhouse. The thump of the ovoids falling was followed by a white, streaming fog in the very dim light. He withdrew quickly, closing the bunkhouse door behind him and pulling across the outer bolt.

'That should fix them,' the leader muttered. 'Now for the rest of it.'

He crossed the yard swiftly with his three comrades beside him. They found the living-room window partly open. Carefully the four men clambered through it, afterwards hurrying across to the darkness of the hall.

To locate the bedroom doors was simple enough. In the first bedroom two dim figures were visible, sleeping soundly after their long sojourn in the open air.

'Shut the window, Clem, and lock it,' the leader whispered. 'No use lettin' the gas escape. An' no sounds.'

Clem closed the slightly open window and latched it, afterwards moving back to the door. The leader searched for a key in the door and failed to discover one, then took a bomb from the satchel of the man beside him.

He tossed it, waited to see it explode in soft white mist, then withdrew hurriedly and closed the door.

'Now the fat guy,' he said quickly, and the four moved to the next doorway along the narrow passageway.

Within the room, the window slightly open as in the case of Bart and Jane's room, Meredith lay sleeping soundly. He failed to hear the window being locked, but he did awaken abruptly at the sound of the gas bomb hitting the wooden floor. For a second or two he could not fathom events. He heard the door-latch click, saw white mist rising from the end of the bed, then as he breathed in the gas his head swam giddily.

He snatched up the sheet and wound it round his mouth and nostrils, holding his breath. He stumbled over to the window, whipped up the chair from beside it, and smashed out the glass furiously. This done, he searched around the floor until he found a metallic ovoid split into two sections by a hinge. He hurled it outside.

He cast the sheet from his face and stared into the darkness of the yard. He saw a sudden flicker of flame to his right, accompanied by drifting smoke. Through it he caught a momentary glimpse of four figures. He turned and blundered to his gun on the dressing-table, snatched it up, went back to the window, and fired off a shot. The figures had vanished, and in any case smoke was blinding his vision as the fire began to get a hold.

What had happened to Bart and Jane? With a gasp he lumbered outside into the passage to find it filled with a mixture of smoke and sense-deadening gas.

Hands to his mouth and nostrils, he found his way through the doorway into their room. The gas was overwhelming in the confined space, and he felt his legs turn to lead. Dazed, he reeled back into the passage; then holding his breath he tried again. As he had done in his own room, he flung a chair through the window and then turned to the motionless bodies in the bed.

He got Jane as far as the floor, then had to retreat again to get his breath. So, by coming and going, the force of the gas weakening as the fresh air came in, he managed to drag out first Jane, and then Bart, into the corridor. Here he left them for the moment and, his senses steadying again, raced outside in his bare feet.

The fire, started under the pillars of the ranch house flooring, was eating furiously into the side of the sun-dried boarding. Meredith looked at the silent bunkhouse. Unlikely to be any help from there. Suddenly his eyes gleamed.

Twenty yards away, perched eight feet in the air on four massive props, was the vast water-barrel used by the ranch for water supplies. Meredith charged over to it, and climbed up the ladder to the top of the water-barrel. Using his gun, he fired at the steel band that held the upper part of the barrel's staves in position. At the last shot the band gave way, and as Meredith had calculated, the nearly full barrel discharged its contents in a deluge, pouring a miniature tidal wave down against the side of the ranch and obliterating the fire in one mighty explosion of steam.

He came down the ladder and waded through the pools and mud back into the house. In the smoke-filled corridor he found Bart and Jane stirring back into life. By the time he had dragged them into the living-room and lighted the oil-lamps they were almost recovered.

'What the hell's happening?' Bart demanded, settling Jane in a chair as she rubbed her eyes bemusedly.

'An attack, son – and a fire. Fortunately I extinguished the flames.' Meredith went on to explain the details.

'But if it was gas we'd have been dead by now,' Bart protested. 'Same as Cardish and Cook.'

'I'll explain later, son.' Meredith hurried out of the room and returned presently in slippers and his big flannel dressing-gown. With him he carried the gowns of Bart and Jane for them to slip over their flimsy night-attire. Without a word he hurried out again. When he returned a few minutes later he had a hinged object like an Easter egg in his hand.

'I went to the bunkhouse to reassure myself as to the safety of the boys,' he explained. 'They'll be OK now they are recovering. And this object is a clumsy discharged bomb, the kind that was used on us.'

'Why weren't we killed by that gas?' Bart asked.

'Nitrous oxide does not kill, son; it is merely an anaesthetic. Laughing gas, in other words.'

'How the hell do you know it was nitrous oxide?'

'It is one of the few gases which are tasteless and odourless, though I imagine it was mixed with something else which caused the white mist. That helped to prevent the nitrous oxide escaping. The idea, I think, was to put us out long enough for fire to get a hold. Maybe the bunkhouse would have been fired too, only my throwing a bomb in the yard and firing a shot warned the attackers that I, at least, was alert.'

'Why couldn't they have used the same gas they did before?' Bart muttered. 'Why mess about with fire?'

'I think they were aware of the danger to themselves. Sulphuretted hydrogen gas is extremely deadly. Working in the confined space of a room, they also stood the chance of being killed – so they used something less potent . . .' Meredith picked up the hinged egg from the table and examined it. 'The glass fragments reveal that the gas was sealed inside the glass and that again inside the case. The slightest impact dislodged the catch and smashed the glass, releasing the gaseous contents. All very ingenious.'

Bart, who had been pacing restlessly, sat down slowly and gave his father a serious glance.

'Thanks a million for everything you did, Dad. You undoubtedly saved everybody's life – and the stunt with the water-barrel was inspired.'

Jane went across and threw her arms around Meredith's fat neck, kissing him.

'That goes for me too, Randle.'

'I merely endeavoured to show presence of mind, Miss Jane,' Meredith murmured, slightly embarrassed. Jane returned to her seat, then said:

'Evidently we were followed after all.'

'Yes, the battle is joined,' Meredith said gravely. 'Somebody is ruthlessly determined to dispose of us because we are beginning to find out too much.'

'You spoke of sulphuretted hydrogen gas not being safe in an enclosed room,' Bart remarked, thinking. 'I assume that Cook and Cardish both got the works in the open?'

'They must have done,' Meredith agreed. Then his expression hardened. 'This latest revelation of nitrous oxide has, in a sense, helped my deductions immensely. The main elements in this criminal onslaught have been gas, phosphorescence, gliders, and now nitrous oxide. All of which point to a chemist and scientist of considerable skill, even to the point of making small but effective bombs. Formerly we leaned to the opinion that the Reverend Peregrine might be mixed up in it, but he seems to have been nothing but a cat's-paw. Which leaves us with only one other likely culprit.'

Bart frowned. 'Who?'

'I'm thinking of a man who has had training in Denver as a chemist,' Meredith smiled grimly. 'One who is an expert in physics, anatomy, and kindred subjects. He informed us – after only a cursory examination – that both Cook and Cardish had died from sulphuretted hydrogen gas poisoning.'

'Great heavens, you don't mean Dr Adey?' Bart gasped.

'I'm afraid I do, son – yes.'

'But that's absurd!' Jane protested. 'Dr Adey's a trusted and respected doctor.'

'Merely an act to cover himself. The fact remains glaringly obvious that all the behind-the-scenes work in these crimes points to a skilled chemist, and only Dr Adey fulfils that requirement . . . I admit that somewhere in the mountains there may be an equally clever person whom we have not met – but that would not explain away Dr Adey's uncanny certainty as to how death was caused. Further, it seems obvious that somebody in the town is aware in advance of many of our movements. Then again, there was Adey's rather off hand statement that "Hold-up" Hogan had been chloroformed, a fact he deduced from the respiration of the gentleman concerned – long after the event. That was when I first suspected Adey.'

'But wouldn't that defeat his own ends? Apparently Hogan had been a scapegoat, and—'

'Yes, indeed, but some bad timing upset things when the body of Cardish was dropped. From then on it was Adey's best policy to work with us, not against us. Incidentally, chloroform is again a doctor's stock-in-trade. You will recall he suggested a posse. The reason he wanted to join it was so that he might have led us to our deaths, which was why I vetoed the idea and suggested you and I, son, should explore alone . . .'

There was a long silence, then Bart sighed. 'I don't see how we can prove any of this.'

'Oh, there *is* a way.' Meredith smiled complacently. 'I think it would be as well to postpone the intended invasion of the mountains for the moment, until I have more details. This affair tonight shows how easily we might walk into trouble. In the meantime I will tackle Dr Adey personally and see what I can discover – in my own way.'

'Up to you,' Bart shrugged. 'But I don't see what you can do.'

Meredith merely smiled mysteriously and changed the subject.

'I suggest we try and catch up on our interrupted slumbers. I have already detailed two of the bunkhouse men to remain rigidly on guard.'

5

FORCED CONFESSION

Next morning, Meredith rode into town on his familiar grey stallion, attired as usual in his check shirt, riding-pants and Homburg hat, his. 38 holstered in the belt about his enormous middle. He inclined his head gravely at the friendly nods greeting him from the boardwalk, but was prepared for instant action if necessary. If the attackers were aware by now that he, Bart and Jane were still alive, anything might happen.

But nothing did. He rode on as he did every morning – respected mayor of the town. On this occasion, however, he continued going until he reached the abode of Dr Adey. He left his stallion at the gatepost and walked up to the front door. Adey's housekeeper appeared following his knock.

'Good morning, Mayor. Want to see the doctor about poor Mr Cardish, I suppose?'

'I certainly have business with him, madam,' Meredith agreed. 'He's at home?'

'In the surgery. Please go in.'

Meredith removed his Homburg and stepped into the hall. He opened the surgery door, taking good care to surreptitiously lock it behind him, slipping the key into his pocket. Adey was working at his desk, apparently filling out reports. He glanced once and nodded amiably, then presently he rose.

'Well, Mr Mayor, you're an early visitor. Connected with the recent murders, I suppose?'

'In a way, yes,' Meredith agreed affably. 'But since all of them have been buried and their deaths designated as murder by persons unknown, they are not the prime reason for my being here. I have other urgent business.'

'Oh?' Adey looked surprised. 'Have a seat, anyway.' Meredith nodded and sat down, putting his Homburg carefully under the chair.

'I am here to seek your professional opinion,' he added. 'I have a curious pain in my chest, Doctor.'

Adey smiled. 'You have? Touch of indigestion, maybe. I'll see how things are.' He picked up his stethoscope from the instrument stand and clipped it on his ears. Meredith sat immobile for a moment or two, then as both Adey's hands were busy holding the stethoscope and tapping Meredith's chest the doctor suddenly found his wrists encircled with the steel manacles of handcuffs. As they clicked sharply into place he stared blankly and straightened up.

'What the hell—?'

'Just a precaution, my dear doctor. You will find them extremely hampering if you try and reach for your gun. As for my chest, it was never better.' Meredith got on his feet again, his chubby face determined. 'Sit down, Doctor.'

Baffled, Adey obeyed. He pulled the stethoscope from his ears and flung it on the stand, then he stared at the handcuffs, and presently at Meredith's levelled .38.

'I'm here, doctor, to extract a few home truths,' Meredith explained calmly.

'Dammit, man, have you gone mad?' Adey said bitterly. 'What the hell are you talking about?'

'Insanity is one of the few misfortunes which has not befallen me.' Meredith beamed. 'Suppose we cut to the chase, Doctor . . . What are you looking for in the mountains?'

'What am I. . . ?' Adey stared. 'You *are* mad!'

'You are not doing it very well, Doctor.' Meredith seated himself and kept his gun ready. 'I have gone through a system of elimination of suspects, and there is no longer any doubt that the man with the brains behind much of the crime in this town is you. Whether you wish to admit the fact of your own free will, or whether I must force it out of you, is up to you.' A dangerous glint came into his baby-blue eyes. 'Murder is bad enough, when it involves two innocent men and a young girl – plus the effort to deflect blame on to an uncouth but entirely innocent outlaw; but when it comes to gas bombs and trying to burn people to death, as happened last night at the Flying F, the time for action has come. Now, what's the answer?'

Adey smiled cynically. 'I would suggest, as a doctor, that you have been out in the sun too long, Mr Mayor.'

Meredith shrugged. He got to his feet and surveyed the bottles on the shelf nearby.

'Ammonia, peroxide, nitric acid . . .' Meredith murmured the titles as he studied them. 'Ah yes, nitric acid. Very useful.'

'How – useful?' Adey asked, a catch in his voice.

Meredith smiled and unfastened the vivid scarlet kerchief from about his throat. Suddenly he whisked the kerchief forward, enveloped Adey's face completely and drew it tight over his eyes, blindfolding him. Adey tried to leap to his feet, but strong hands bumped him down again into the chair. The next thing he knew, his handcuffed wrists were being fastened with cord to one arm of the chair, then his left ankle was treated to a similar shackling, being secured to the chair's left leg. His right one, to his surprise, was left free.

'Comfortable, Doctor?' asked Meredith's cold voice.

'I'll have you kicked out of town for this assault, Mayor,' Adey panted, from amidst the kerchief's folds. 'What the blazes do you think you're doing?'

'I am considering how full is this bottle of nitric acid.' Meredith took the bottle down and put it on the bench. After a moment or two he put it back in its place and turned on the hot-water tap in the sink very slightly, leaving it running.

'What's the idea?' Adey panted, kicking his free foot desperately. 'What do you *want*?'

'The facts, so I may know how to act. I only need your verification. I hold the whip hand. I am giving you a chance to tell us everything, verify the story which is known also by now to the sheriff and, of course, his wife. He will act the moment I have your admission. You are behind the recent murders, make no mistake about it, and whatever is going on in the way of phantoms and dirty work is your doing. I'll give you sixty seconds to make up your mind to confess.'

'And suppose I still say you're crazy?'

'In that case I shall be forced to the odious necessity of extracting information by means of pouring nitric add over your bare foot. You leave me no alternative.'

'Good God, man, you wouldn't—'

'I'm afraid I would,' Meredith said calmly, his eyes on the steam rising from the still-running hot water. The water made scarcely any sound in the sink, so gently was it flowing.

'I've nothing to tell!' Adey panted, struggling uselessly to free himself.

'If I may take off your shoe, sir,' Meredith murmured, and he unlaced it swiftly and tugged it off. The sock followed. Then with a considerable amount of noise he found an enamel bowl and put it on the floor. Adey gave a yelp as his foot touched the icy bowl.

'The nitric acid is not yet there, sir,' Meredith said drily. 'How long it will be delayed depends on you. I think I am right in asserting that you are mixed up with some kind of gang that has found something extremely valuable in the mountains, that your knowledge of science and medicine has proved useful in producing a ghost and enabling several murders. Is not that so?'

Adey muttered a muffled obscenity. Meredith shrugged to himself and turned to the nitric acid bottle. He pulled out the cork with a squeegeeing *thonk!* and then put it gently back in the neck again and returned it to the shelf. Next he picked up a tin cup, and filled it with hot water.

'Last chance, sir,' he said coldly.

Adey did not speak, but he yelled desperately as several drops of scalding water spattered over his bare foot. He yelled all the more when Meredith seized his leg firmly and forced his foot into the enamel bowl. A few more drops spattered. . . .

'You're right!' Adey yelled. 'For God's sake, Mayor, keep that acid away! You're right, damn you!'

'About what?' Meredith asked levelly.

'I – I am connected with a – wealthy backer. I—'

'You mean that you are not the head of this illegal gang? That you are merely an underling?'

'I'm not a damned underling!' Adey snapped. More

scalding drops descended on his foot as Adey hesitated. Then he began talking quickly.

'A few months ago I . . . I was in the mountains, pursuing my hobby of climbing, when I discovered a bronze door set into a cave entrance. I returned with explosives and blew it open. Inside the cave I found inscriptions and drawings chiselled into a slab set in the wall. At back of the cave there was clearly a large tunnel going back into the mountains, but it was completely blocked with boulders and stones. I recognized the inscriptions as being Indian, but I could make nothing of them. I sensed they might be important so I made a careful copy of them by tracing the indentations.' Adey fell silent.

'Go on, Doctor. This is most fascinating. A little more acid?' Meredith murmured, as Adey still hesitated, wriggling desperately. The threat loosened his tongue again.

'I sent them to someone I'd known in Denver, an expert in Apache and Navajo history. He immediately wrote back, telling me they were Navajo symbols, left behind from the dynasty the Navajo Indians once possessed in this state – and others. They were a mighty race in their time, and he suspected that they had left behind hidden treasures – silver, precious stones, and heaven knows what. The inscription was a sort of curse, warning anyone to stay away from their treasures and sacred site . . .'

'The Halls of Manuza?' Meredith murmured. 'The tunnels to which they had blocked off?'

'How the hell do you know that?' Adey gasped.

'Never mind how I know, Doctor. Now let me guess the rest. Your backer offered you a fortune if you could recover and illegally remove these ancient treasures, which he would fence to private buyers, rather than let them go to some museum. You entrusted your secret to a handful of men, and began trying to remove the rock barrier. You could not risk using more explosives for fear of attracting attention, not to mention the risk of bringing down the tunnels themselves and burying the treasures for ever. You had to do everything by hand, and the barrier was extensive. So your backer sent in his own army of thugs to augment your small labour force – and bring them fresh provisions.

'So, carrying on as the genial town doctor, you launched robbery with violence,' Meredith continued, icy contempt in his voice. 'You have engineered what amounts to a mining operation – or archaeological dig – in the mountains, and kept people away – scared them away in fact – by murder, faked ghosts, and similar hocus pocus. I'm right, aren't I? *Aren't I?*' Meredith allowed a few more scalding hot drops to drop on to Adey's foot.

'*Stop it!*' he yelled. 'Yes! Let me go – I've told you every-thing~—'

'Not quite everything. For instance, I wish you to verify that the bodies of Cardish and Cook were dropped from a glider.'

'They – they were. I had – and still have at night – guards along the trail to the mountains. Any curiosity-monger is dealt with ruthlessly, if not by the guards then by the ghost rider who prowls by night. With those two men it was the ghost rider himself who acted on each occasion. He overpowered both men by gassing them – to leave no bullet trace. They were then transported to the nearest mountain glider base, then dumped to make the murders look supernatural.'

'And bad timing in the case of Cardish upset your neat little plan to blot out Hogan, whom you'd selected as a scapegoat, didn't it?' Meredith demanded. '*Didn't it?*'

'Yes,' Adey gasped. 'With matters getting rather warm, I

thought Hogan was the most likely man to whom blame could attach – since I didn't seem able to pin anything on the other newcomer, the Reverend Peregrine. But, as you say, Cardish was returned too abruptly, and it proved Hogan innocent. From then on the heat definitely turned in my direction.'

'And you deliberately killed Babs Armstrong just to turn Hogan into a scapegoat?' Meredith asked, with dangerous quietness.

'I had a double motive,' Adey responded. 'That girl was the inquisitive sort. She knew quite a deal about my activities – far too much, so I had to settle her once and for all. It was simple enough. After leaving the dance she called to see me. I had asked her to do so to pick up some medicine for her father. A correctly timed blow, with my knowledge of anatomy, broke her neck. My home is some way down the main street – so it was simple to get her in the street before anybody else came along.

'Hogan, of course, I had singled out earlier as a cat's-paw . . . I had one of my men watch him. Acting on my orders, the man tackled Hogan that night on the trail, overpowered and chloroformed him. He was brought back to my surgery, unconscious. Then when Babs Armstrong was dealt with, Hogan, just on the point of recovering, was thrown on top of her. All a matter of swift action and careful timing.'

Notwithstanding his reluctance to incriminate himself, Adey's egotism had compelled him to boast of his elaborate schemes. Meredith compressed his lips.

'In fact, Adey, you are several kinds of disgusting sadist, are you not?' he said then.

'I think not, Mayor. A sadist inflicts misery and death for the joy of it; I have merely blotted out everything likely to hinder my finding an incalculably wealthy treasure. Now, untie me!'

'We're not finished yet,' Meredith said. 'Was it you who fired at us from the glider when we were last in the mountains?'

'It must have been one of the guards. I was in town.'

'And what super criminal is to be the receiver of all this illegal treasure?' Meredith questioned.

'You can go to hell!' Adey snapped. 'I'll—'

Adey broke off, and his head inside the kerchief turned as there was a sudden splintering of glass from the high window. Meredith twirled too, diving for his gun, but he was not quite quick enough. The barrel of a .38 was pointing at him.

'Get your hands up, Mayor!' a voice commanded from the broken window. Meredith obeyed slowly and turned. The gunman slammed up the sash and came clambering down on to the bench. Still keeping Meredith covered he advanced to the door, then found the key was missing. 'All right, where is it?' he snapped, coming forward.

Meredith lowered his hand to his shirt pocket, but the gunman was suspicious of the action. He found the key for himself, opened the door, and admitted the housekeeper. Meredith surveyed her curiously. She was no longer the plump, pleasant woman she usually seemed. Her face was viciously set, and a .32 was aimed steadily in her hand.

Meredith cursed himself for not having suspected her when he had gained admittance. She was probably Adey's mistress, and naturally he would have confided in her.

'I gather, madam, you overheard my conversation with the doctor?' Meredith enquired blandly.

'I heard the Doctor shouting,' the woman retorted. 'I figured it was about time he got some help.' She crossed over to Adey and tore the kerchief from his face. Then she went to work unfastening the cords as he stared anxiously at his bare foot and leg. He frowned as he beheld nothing but water splashes.

'Hot water, my dear Doctor, plus imagination,' Meredith explained, gesturing with his raised hand. 'Thank you for telling me as much as you did. A pity we were interrupted at the most interesting point.'

'Get these handcuffs off,' Adey snapped, glaring. Meredith lowered his hands and then put them up again as the .38 jabbed him.

'Just keep those hands to yourself, Homburg,' the gunman advised. 'Which pocket has the key?'

'Left shirt-pocket – and be careful. I am somewhat ticklish. The gunman grinned sourly and dug his hand in the pocket – then he fancied a sudden earthquake struck him. Meredith had waited for the one hand to be imprisoned and the gun aim deflected. Now he jammed forth his enormous stomach with all his strength, and the sudden impact winded the gunman completely. A second later a fist slammed under his jaw and sent him flying backwards into the housekeeper with the .32. She staggered a few paces, and as nimbly as a ballet dancer Meredith darted across the surgery and snatched the .32 from her – only to drop it as the gunman recovered abruptly and got in a lucky right hook.

Helplessly, Meredith rocked on his heels, and before he could recover his balance a chair crashed down brutally across the top of his head. Dazed, he sank to the floor, his vision blurred and his head singing. The handcuff key was dragged from his shirt pocket, and with a sudden click Adey found himself free. He stood up and scooped back his disordered hair.

'Now, Mr Mayor, it's my turn,' he said coldly, levelling Meredith's own .38. 'Get on your feet. The misfortune about all this business is that you have told your precious theories to the sheriff, who in turn will spread them all around the neighbourhood. I am no longer in a safe position,' Adey continued, 'so I must come into the open. I suppose it would have come about sooner or later in any case. The only thing to do, if I am to resume my normal occupation as a doctor, and remain the power behind the – er – activities in the mountains, is to be rid of you, and afterwards the sheriff and his precious wife.'

Adey glanced at the gunman. 'Get the buckboard, Steve, and bring it to the back door. Collect three of the boys as well and a length of rope.'

'You figurin' on a necktie party, Doc?' Steve asked uneasily. 'Isn't that dangerous around here?'

'I'm planning an accident,' Adey retorted. 'I intend to be rid of Mayor Meredith most effectually.' Whilst the gunman kept Meredith covered with his .38, Adey drew on his sock and laced up his shoe.

'Accident?' Steve repeatedly obtusely. 'Why?'

'Because, you fool, I don't want anything traced back to me. You'll get the buckboard, as I told you, together with some of the boys, and take the mayor here out to Graveyard Canyon. Get the horses free of the wagon and then send it over the cliff with Meredith inside it. When he's hit bottom follow on down to the spot, untie the ropes which will have been binding him, and also leave the horses there. When he's found it'll look as though the mayor here plunged over the cliff and was killed. The horses could have broken clear of the shafts and escaped injury. Understand?'

'Sure thing,' Steve agreed. 'I'll get the buckboard right now.'

'And hurry it up,' Adey snapped. 'No telling how soon the sheriff may come along, wondering what's happened to the mayor here.'

Steve hurried out, and Adey looked back at Meredith. His huge, round face was expressionless. Stooping, Adey retrieved Meredith's Homburg from the floor and jammed it back on his head. 'Your body may not be recognizable after your fall into the canyon,' he said drily. 'Not so clever as you thought, Mayor, eh?'

'All of us are liable to miscalculations.' Meredith sighed. 'A word of warning, however. When I escape from this present predicament – not if – I shall consider it my bounden duty to hound you to the ends of the earth if need be until justice is done. Since you are thrice, and maybe more times, a murderer, you will have to pay the penalty, sooner or later.'

'You certainly talk a lot, my friend,' Adey commented drily. 'But soon, you will be silenced for ever.'

Meredith had no opportunity to respond, for at that moment Steve returned, accompanied by three other roughnecks, one of them holding a rope. Helpless, Meredith submitted to being firmly bound about the wrists and ankles. Lastly he was gagged, and then by dint of a good deal of effort the four gunmen between them carried his eighteen stone plus to the back yard and dumped him in the waiting buckboard. Red-faced and panting they looked at Dr Adey, who had followed them out. He handed them some tarpaulin sheeting.

'Cover him with this,' he ordered. 'You can hardly ride through the town with him in full view.'

Meredith, curled up in the buckboard like an over-stuffed bolster, found himself suddenly smothered under the sheeting. He made no effort to push it on one side, and after a moment or two the creak of the wheels and the jolting of the wagon satisfied him that the journey to Graveyard Canyon had commenced.

*

Bart came to a sudden halt in his restless pacing of the ranch house living-room. Jane was seated nearby. Outside could be heard the noise of the bunkhouse boys repairing the fire damage of the night before and reconstructing the shattered water-butt.

'I don't like it, Jane! It's all very well for Dad to sail into the fight by himself, just so he can be unorthodox, and mebbe outside the law – but what happens if anything goes wrong?'

Jane shrugged. 'Since he asked for a clear field, I think he ought to have it. He said don't go into town in the usual way but give him until noon; then if nothing happened you could start to investigate. It needs more than an hour yet.'

'But suppose, for instance, that Dad is wrong in his notions about Dr Adey? It might start a hell of a row . . .'

'Talk of the devil,' Jane said quickly, looking through the window. 'Here is Dr Adey now!'

'Huh?' Bart joined her at the window. 'He seems to be alone. Is it coincidence, or is something brewing?'

'Nothing he can do on his own, with all the boys of the outfit around the place. Better let him in, Bart, he's coming across the yard now.'

When Bart opened the outer screen door he found Adey just tying his horse to the porch tie rack.

'Hello, Sheriff!' Adey called up genially, tugging off his Stetson as he came ups the steps.

' 'Morning,' Bart answered suspiciously. 'Anything wrong? You'd better come in.'

Both men had come into the living-room before Adey blandly explained himself after nodding to the puzzled Jane.

'I'm here because I couldn't find you at your office as usual this morning, Sheriff. I wanted to hand you these detailed medical reports on the deaths of Cook, Cardish, and Babs Armstrong.' From his wallet he produced three separate sheets of folded foolscap and put them down on the table.

'I – er – was delayed leaving,' Bart said.

'I see.' Silence. Jane and Bart glanced at each other.

'Haven't you seen the mayor?' Jane asked abruptly.

'Mr Meredith? Why, no. Should I have done?'

Looking through the window, Jane suddenly gave a gasp of alarm.

'Bart! Look! A bunch of horsemen tackling our boys . . .'

Before Bart could move, he was checked by Adey's gun suddenly leaping into his hand.

'Come over here, Mrs Meredith!' he snapped. 'You, Sheriff, stay right where you are.'

'So Dad guessed right!' Bart said bitterly. '*You* are the man we've been looking for!'

Adey smiled coldly. 'I'd be a fool to admit anything, Sheriff. I will tell you, however that I came in advance of my men to hold your attention whilst they deal with the members of your ranch outfit. Then I intend to make a more thorough job of the effort my boys bungled last night.'

'You mean to burn the place with us in it?' Jane whispered.

'Precisely. By doing that no blame can possibly attach to me, since any ranch can catch fire – and often does. You both know too much about me for comfort . . .'

Adey broke off and glanced towards the door as it opened suddenly and one of his own men, gun in hand, came in.

'We've taken care of the outfit, Doc. Whole damned bunch is hog-tied in the bunkhouse. Reckon if we set fire to the spread they'll go up with it as well.'

'There are fifteen men in there!' Jane cried in horror.

Adey ignored her. 'All right, Clem,' he added to the gun-hawk, 'get the ropes and tie these two up.'

Bart took an angry step forward but stopped as Adey's gun menaced him.

'I don't want to shoot you, and leave a tell-tale bullet behind,' he said, 'but I won't hesitate if you try anything. None of this would have been necessary had you kept your nose out of my affairs. The mayor has already paid the price, and now it's your turn. As for the boys in the bunkhouse, it's their hard luck that they are mixed up with you.'

Bart breathed hard, Jane clinging to his arm. Clem came back with a long length of tough rope, and under Adey's directions he secured Bart and Jane, facing away from each other, to two upright pillars supporting the living-room roof.

'Everything's ready, boss,' Clem said, eager to make up for his failure the previous night. 'There's hay and straw under the bunkhouse an' the spread here. The whole lot'll go up like a fire-cracker.'

'Good enough,' Adey said. Bart and Jane heard the door slam as they left. Desperately Bart struggled to tear free of the ropes holding him, but the knots only tightened. Then Jane's horrified voice reached him.

'Bart, they've done it! Smoke is coming up through the floorboards . . .'

She broke off in a fit of coughing as the first wisps of it were drawn into her lungs.

Bart renewed his efforts at tearing himself free, but had to desist from sheer exhaustion. Steve was certainly no novice when it came to knot-tying.

'Bart!' Jane screamed. 'The whole place will be ablaze any minute . . .'

She was right. Through the cracks in the floorboards smoke and little spurts of flame were appearing. So far the fire seemed to be confined to the further end of the living-room, but before long the entire place would become a raging inferno.

'Nothing I can do, Jane,' Bart panted hoarsely in the smoke. 'These damned knots won't—'

He broke off as there was a sudden rending and crack-ing of boards. Jane shuddered as she imagined it was the fire breaking through; then to her amazement she heard a voice in her ear.

'Take it easy, ma'am. We'll soon get you out of this.'

The next moment the ropes tightly holding Jane gave way as a knife-blade cut through them quickly. She turned, her eyes smarting with smoke, to find the bristly, grim face of "Hold-up" Hogan standing behind her.

'*You!*' she gasped incredulously.

'Me an' the Reverend,' he said. He nodded to where Peregrine was rapidly freeing an equally astonished Bart.

'Quickly – back out the way we came in,' the Reverend said. 'Under the flooring. The fire has not got that far yet . . .' He led the way through the smoke, away from where the flames were beginning to get a hold on the further end of the room.

Part of the floor had been smashed upwards. They dropped into the space below, then wriggled their way along on hands and knees away from the fire some twenty feet behind them. Then they were free of the confined, smoke-filled area and stumbled to their feet in the yard not far from the blazing bunkhouse.

'There are fifteen men bound up in there!' Jane cried. 'They'll be—'

'They're over there,' the Reverend said, and nodded to one of the stables well separated from the holocaust. 'And that is where we are going, shielded by this smoke. Dr Adey and his boys are still at the front, watching the blaze. We will receive bullets if we're seen. Come . . .'

He led the way quickly through the smoke clouds, Bart, Jane, and the burly outlaw coming up in the rear. When they entered the big stable they found the boys of the outfit all there, grim and dishevelled.

'Are we just goin' to let this dirty skunk Adey get away with this, Mr Meredith?' demanded Kevin Briggs, the foreman. 'The whole durned place is goin' up in flames! This stable, separate from the rest, is about the only place in the clear.'

'The ranch house and bunkhouse can be replaced, Kev – lives can't,' Bart answered briefly. 'Adey is intent on watching this blaze. If we go outside and he sees us that's the end of everything. But how did you turn up as you did, Reverend – and you, Hogan?'

'Reckon I just tacked along with the Reverend,' Hogan growled. 'Don't say 'cos I've robbed trains and stages that I'm a no-account skunk as well. When them folks in the town was all set for hangin' me, I guess you an' Mr Meredith was the only ones who tried to save me. Now I've repaid you. But you can thank the Reverend for gettin' you rescued.'

'I followed Adey,' Peregrine explained. 'I was about to call upon the doctor concerning my indigestion, when I saw him leaving his home on horseback. A little while later I saw Hogan here, riding alone and aimlessly in the main street. I decided that it might be a good chance for me to try and start converting him to my Gospel. It was in the course of conversation that he mentioned he had seen the doctor and a gang of men riding out along the trail. The sudden addition of a gang of men, and with the *doctor*, puzzled me. I decided to follow, and Hogan accompanied me. We were just in time to see this gang of men over-powering the members of your outfit, Sheriff.' The cleric paused and gave a shrug.

'There was no sign of the doctor, but we knew he was around by the presence of his horse. The gang was preoc-cupied at the bunkhouse so, quite unnoticed, we hid ourselves under the ranch floor. Easy enough since it's on stilts. The rest you know. We forced our way through loose boards to your aid, having overheard all that was intended.'

'And saved our lives,' Bart said quietly. 'I can never thank you enough for that, Reverend. I certainly don't need any more proof that you're as innocent of crime as my wife here.'

'But of course I am,' Peregrine exclaimed. 'The fault lies with the men who call themselves my followers. I'm afraid they have betrayed me . . . but I shall gather others to my side in time. True, loyal devotees of the Gospel.' He peered outside at the blazing shell of the ranch house. 'I fear that your home is a total loss, Sheriff,' he commented, sighing. 'And the bunkhouse, too.'

'We'll rebuild it later,' Bart muttered. 'Live somewhere else in the meantime.' He looked over Peregrine's shoul-der and through the smoke-wreaths. 'Apparently Adey and his men have gone, well satisfied with their handi-work.'

'And we're supposed to be dead,' Jane put in. 'Maybe that gives us an advantage.'

'What do you suppose has happened to Dad?' Bart asked grimly. 'Adey said he'd "been taken care of", which means—' Bart broke off thickly. 'If Dad's dead on account of Adey, I'll kill that dirty swine myself and then take the consequences.'

There was silence for a moment, even from the outfit at

the rear of the stable; then the Reverend cleared his throat gently.

'Your emotions are understandable, sir. Though I do not admit violence into my creed, I must confess that at times there seems to be justification for it.'

'I'm not interested in justification, Reverend – only revenge! Dad was also my best friend. I'll avenge him, even if I put a rope around my own neck.'

'We will all avenge him,' Peregrine said. 'The town must be rid of this man Adey, and everything he stands for. He is now revealed in his true colours.'

'And unless we can act he'll go right on as the doctor tending the sick,' Jane remarked acidly.

'We must act with caution. For the time being you have to find a new home, with friends you can trust who will not be likely to give away the fact that you are still alive . . .'

'Maybe Bill Hardwick at the Triple G will fix us up,' Bart said. 'The sooner we ride over to his ranch the better. The horses are all right, thank heaven, so let's get moving. I'll have to make arrangements to round up my cattle for the time being, too; maybe leaving you to do it, Reverend. Just as long as Jane and I don't appear. Once those details are out of the way, I can concentrate on avenging Dad.'

6

MEREDITH ESCAPES

The bumping, rattling journey to Graveyard Canyon was not far from its end – though, under the tarpaulin, Randle Meredith was not aware of it. He was far too busy working on the ropes binding his wrists. In the side of the buckboard was the end of a nail, perhaps an inch of it, which had been driven through the planking and not been flattened afterwards. He had discovered it in the first place when the jolting of the wagon had hurled him against it. Now he had the knot about his wrists firmly jammed on the point and was tugging and straining savagely.

It was not long before his efforts were rewarded and he felt his wrists suddenly free. Thanking heaven for the concealment of the tarpaulin, he unfastened his ankles and then raised the edge of the sheeting gently and peered outside.

The looming face of the mountain greeted him as the buckboard pursued a rattling, shaking course along a curving trail – going ever higher.

On the driving-seat sat Steve, busy with the reins and whip, whilst on either side of him were two of his rough-neck companions. The fourth man was in the buckboard itself, but he was not watching Meredith. Like the trio on the driving-seat he was looking frontward, quite satisfied that his captive was unable to free himself. Meredith surveyed this scene surreptitiously, and then vanished again under the tarpaulin.

Very carefully he began sliding himself backwards towards the buckboard's open end. Since the tarpaulin was naturally stiff it remained in a fixed position in spite of his movements. Presently he realized his legs had left the boarding and were dangling in emptiness. He slid still further until he felt the trail fling his feet from under him. He was debating whether or not to let himself go when the wagon suddenly swung fiercely to the left round a bend.

Meredith was flung from his precarious hold and crashed helplessly into stones and dust, rolling over and over heavily. Any sounds were drowned by the din of the wheels, rattling on the loose stones. By the time he had come to rest on a long slope, after a further long roll broken by the presence of a thick mountain bush, the wagon was out of sight round the bend in the trail, the tarpaulin still undisturbed by reason of its unyielding stiff-ness.

Dislodging his enormous girth from the bush Meredith heaved to his feet, swaying on the steeply shelving bank. He thought of returning to the trail, then changed his mind. Steve and the boys might discover at any moment that they had lost their victim and come searching – so, slipping and stumbling, Meredith went down the slope and finished up amidst a cluster of towering rocks. He looked about him.

He was completely lost. Though in the time he had

lived in the district he had explored a good deal of it, he did not know every twist and turn of this vast range. All he could do was take his position from the sun and, since the Flying F ranch lay due north, strike out in that direction. So, puffing and blowing in the blazing heat, he got on the move. His famous Homburg, still clamped on his head, offered little protection from the searing rays, and his kerchief had been left behind when he tackled Adey. So he tugged off his shirt and fashioned it into a crude head-dress, thereafter tramping on in singlet and riding-pants and devoid of his gun.

At a gurgling freshet tumbling from the heights he refreshed himself and then drew quickly into cover as he caught the sound of hoof-beats somewhere above. From his sanctuary he saw the buckboard moving slowly along the trail, Steve and his boys looking keenly about them. Gradually they rode on out of sight.

So Meredith emerged again, and kept on going north-ward. On foot it was a hard, merciless progress, and Meredith said quite a few things to himself as he walked, not quite in keeping with his usual aplomb. Until at last it dawned on him, towards the middle of the afternoon, that he was not very far from the spot where he and Bart had taken up position during their vigil watching for the ghost-rider. He struggled on again with new heart, always prepared for the return of the buckboard on the trail above.

Another mountain stream, at which he drank and bathed his face and neck, refreshed him. Lack of food did not particularly trouble him. He probably had enough blubber to keep him going for a week. So he toiled on, coming at last within view of the desert trail that led to the Flying F as twilight was beginning to fall.

Rather than risk going on the trail whilst any light

remained, he wedged himself in a niche of the rocks and calmly went to sleep. When he awoke he was shivering with the cold and promptly returned the shirt to his almost naked chest and shoulders.

'Well, I reckon it ain't no use lookin' any more now the night's come. We'd best tell the doc Pot-belly has ditched us. He'll be mad as hell, but there ain't nothin' else we can do.'

Meredith froze as he heard the voice of Steve not very far away; then, realizing the rocks were hiding him, he began to move again. Edging his way round the nearest spur, he presently caught sight of Steve and his three companions outlined against the stars, on a nearby rimrock. Meredith was possessed of only one thought – the buckboard had to be somewhere near at hand! If he could only get hold of that wagon. . . .

He thought fast, as he usually did in a crisis. Feeling around him, he picked up a moderate-sized stone. 'Old gags are usually the most efficient,' he muttered.

He threw the stone as far away from him as he could. It made a considerable noise, striking the rocks and echoing loudly in the confined space and still night air. The men on the rimrock turned suddenly and peered into the darkness.

'What the hell was that?' one of them demanded. Meredith threw another stone – and then another. They made less noise than the first, but they were certainly audible.

'Sounds like—' one of the men began, but Steve cut him short.

'Shut up, you fool!' he whispered. 'If that's Homburg down there, our voices'll carry. Branch out. You two work round the back.'

Eager to avoid having to confess their carelessness to Dr

Adey, the men broke up and began to scramble down the rocky slope. Meredith, well hidden, watched them and grinned to himself. To get down the slope was far easier than getting up it would be. He began to move with silent swiftness and presently gained the rimrock. Down below he could hear the men scrambling amidst the stones.

He threw another small rock in a different direction and then began searching for the horse and buckboard. He came upon it almost immediately, standing at the top of the slope which led down tortuously to the main trail, only a matter of a few yards away from where he and Bart had first seen the ghost rider speeding to attack Jane.

Grunting and puffing, Meredith hauled himself up to the driving-seat and flicked the reins. Immediately the horses got on the move. Bounding and bumping, the wagon thundered violently down the rocky slope until it hit the more or less level ground of the trail. Once here Meredith used the whip and lashed the two animals into all the furious galloping they could muster.

The four gunmen must have heard his departure, but there was nothing they could do about it. By the time they got up the slope he would be out of sight in the darkness. He chuckled to himself and went on driving the team relentlessly, dust clouding up under the spinning wheels.

So Meredith kept going, through a full two-and-a-half-hour ride. By this time the horses were weary and moving at no more than a crawl, and Meredith himself was bruised with the hard wood of the seat and nearly frozen stiff by the cold night wind. He began looking out anxiously for the first signs of the Flying F, then frowned and wondered if he had missed his direction when he failed to detect its dark bulk ahead of him.

He kept on going, sure he was not mistaken in his route – but when he arrived at last at the gutted remains of the spread he just did not know what to think. He clambered down heavily from the driving-seat, fastened the sweating horses to the gatepost, then went across the yard and gazed on the black ashes and charred posts in the starlight. The corrals were empty, the gates swinging. Ranch house and bunkhouse had both disappeared into rubble. Only the stables and a single barn remained intact.

He was struck by a chilling thought. Adey had said he would deal with Bart and Jane, but surely this didn't mean. . . ? For once in his life Meredith felt completely helpless, then gradually his incisive mind got matters into focus again.

'A fire this size must have been seen,' he muttered. 'If not as far away as the town, then certainly by our nearest neighbours at the Triple G. I must find out right away.'

In a matter of perhaps ten minutes he had driven across the dim but mainly level pastureland to the Triple G, speeding straight into the yard. Very nearly breathless with anxiety, he hurried up the porch steps and hammered violently on the screen-door.

It was a moment or two before an oil-lamp appeared and Eve Hardwick, wife of the ranch-owner, opened the screen-door wide.

'Mr Meredith!' she gasped, in relief and amazement. 'Oh, thank heaven! We were just talking about you. We—'

'My son and his wife, madam,' Meredith interrupted, his voice breaking.

'They're here – in the living-room. Come right in.'

'Here?' Meredith expelled a comical sigh of relief, then returned to his normal dignity. 'I never heard sweeter words, madam. Please lead the way.'

Eve Hardwick smiled and turned back into the hall. Meredith followed ponderously behind her, his round face beaming as he entered the living-room. He still managed to maintain his dignity as Bart and Jane leapt up from their chairs and began to pump his hands in eager greeting.

'A memorable moment,' he said, his voice catching a little. 'I am – hmm – glad to think that I might have been missed.'

'Missed!' Bart cried blankly. 'How on earth do you suppose things around here would go on ticking without you? We'd given you up for lost, and were planning to avenge you— That is, Jane and I, and "Hold-up" and the Reverend.'

Surprised, Meredith looked towards the outlaw and the cleric as they sat in the lamplight regarding him, smiling faintly.

'You'll want a meal, Mr Meredith,' Mrs Hardwick said quickly, and bustled into the back regions. Her husband came over from the fireplace, where he had been watching the proceedings.

'And some warmer clothes and food, from the look of you,' he added. 'Come to the fire, Mr Mayor.'

'I thank you, sir.' Meredith moved towards the flames and held out his hands towards them.

'Well, what happened?' Bart asked. 'How did you manage to escape Adey?'

'Partly accident, son; partly intentional.' Meredith gave the details, and by the time he had finished a hot meal had been brought for him, together with coffee. He settled down at the table with the grace of a Falstaff.

'That Navajo treasure sounds interesting,' Bart said, thinking.

'Very interesting, son – but might I ask what happened at the Flying F? I feared you and Jane had been killed, just as you feared I had.'

It was Bart's turn to explain, and he did so in detail.

Meredith nodded slowly as he finished.

'Allow me to add my own thanks, gentlemen,' he said, looking at the Reverend and then Hogan. 'I'm gratified that my judgement of you, Reverend, was correct. I'm afraid you are much too innocent a man to be turned loose among the roughnecks who inhabit this territory . . . Apparently, son,' Meredith glanced at Bart, 'we now have before us the necessity of rebuilding the Flying F yet again?'

'At a later date,' Bart responded. 'Bill here is willing for us to stay at the Triple G until we have dealt with Adey completely. We now have the Reverend and Hogan on our side, which is a help. Another thing in our favour is that Jane and I are believed dead. Same goes for our boys in the outfit, who are digging in with Bill's men for the time being.'

'For my own part,' Meredith said, 'I am known to be alive, of course – or will be when Steve and his unpleasant friends report back. So I do not think there would be much gained by your staying under cover, son. We shall, as usual, act in concert. We may also be sure that the moment Adey hears that I at least am still alive and free he will leave Mountain Peak with all speed and probably join his men in the hills.'

'To where he must be followed,' Bart snapped. 'We've got to smash him, Dad, and everything he's doing.'

'I'm in on this too, as much as any of you,' Jane put in with surprising vehemence. 'Especially after the spread was burned down!'

'Just what do you imagine is happening in the mountains?' Peregrine asked. 'Any conclusions, Mr Mayor?'

'Yes indeed.' Meredith poured himself some coffee and then continued: 'the recent recruitment of that army of thugs and their stealing of supplies suggests that they are still engaged in excavating the tunnels, and have yet to find the treasure. But that will only be a matter of time, unless they are stopped.'

'You mean that Adey recruited my erstwhile flock as miners, and is planning on robbing the Navajo tombs and selling the treasures?' Peregrine asked, thinking.

'That, Reverend, is my guess,' Meredith conceded. 'Adey admitted as much. Permission to excavate in those mountains can only be granted by the authorities of this town – myself and the sheriff – since the town of Mountain Peak owns the mountains. Doubtless he knew in advance that I, at least, would never grant permission without satisfying myself as to the reason for it being wanted. Since the Halls of Manuza are a site of religious and historical interest, I would have contacted the government or some museum, and handed things over to them. Naturally that would still have generated income and benefits to the town.' Meredith took an appreciative sip of his coffee before continuing.

'Rather than take that chance, Adey and his financial backer have begun to work without permission, using an elaborate scare system to keep away prowlers. Had they had only the superstitious country folk of this town to deal with they would have been left undisturbed – but we, from more educated regions, provide serious opposition, hence the effort to be rid of us. And naturally, Dr Adey, himself a scientist of no mean ability, is the – er – town agent of this ruthless gang.'

'Yes, it seems to hang together,' Bart admitted.

'You're lost in this region, Mr Meredith,' Bill Hardwick remarked, smiling. 'You ought to be a chief of detectives or else a college professor.'

'Frankly, sir, the prospect of teaching young people would appal me! I am quite content to have my knowledge and use it where I can. Obviously, our next moves are to stop Adey and his men breaking into the sacred site, and then inform the nearest authorities and have them take action.'

'Wouldn't it be as well to do that in any case?' the Reverend Peregrine suggested. 'It would perhaps save us a lot of dangerous work—'

'In this town, Reverend, we have made it our business to fight our *own* battles,' Meredith said. 'In the past we have had menaces and bad men and, by our own efforts, have cleaned up the trouble. Only by such tactics can a town gain a respected name abroad and build up law and order. There is another point too. If a marshal and his men came over here to investigate they would at the same time ask a lot of questions in which Mr "Hold-up" Hogan here would be involved. As the rescuer of my son and his wife – along with yourself, of course – I do not propose to let him be subject to arrest. No, we will fight this battle ourselves and be all the more self-respecting for it when we've finished.'

'Mmm . . .' The cleric reflected for a moment. 'Forgive me, Mayor, if I say it seems a bit illogical.'

'Of course it is.' Bart grinned. 'But you don't know Dad very well, Reverend. On past occasions when I have tried to bring in the authorities he has stopped me. The real truth is, he loves a fight!'

Meredith considered the ceiling with his innocent blue eyes.

'And usually wins it,' Jane added in admiration. 'I'd back Randle and his brains against all the crooks in existence. And I'm fully in agreement with him. Let's finish the fight ourselves!'

'Thank you, Miss Jane, for those kind words,' Meredith murmured, beaming benevolently.

'Supposin' we win?' Hogan asked, frowning with unaccustomed concentration as he followed the conversation. 'What do we get out of it?'

'Fame, my friend,' Meredith responded. 'Mountain Peak will become a town of note and prosperity. Archaeologists, museum authorities and historians will be sent here by the government to catalogue the treasures, and perhaps eventually remove them to a national museum. We shall reap a harvest, not only from the money they will bring into our expanding town, but also from the finances the government will pay us – the town, anyway – for permitting that to be done.'

'Got it all worked out, as usual,' Bart smiled.

'I always try, son. Our power to grant permission to the government would, incidentally, be considerably weakened if we had to call in the authorities to throw out these usurpers. It would look as though we were too weak to handle our own affairs.' Meredith got up stiffly from the table and flexed his tired limbs.

'What comes next, then?' Bill Hardwick enquired. 'We go into the mountains and attack them?'

Peregrine coughed and asked a question.

'Can I be of further service, Mr Mayor? Conflict is not really my forte, but—'

'I think,' Meredith answered, looking at the cleric and Hogan, 'that it might be politic for both you and Mr Hogan to return to town. If you stay here you might draw attention to this ranch. It would be a useful diversion if you went on with your preaching, with Mr Hogan as your – er – convert.'

Peregrine looked slightly relieved as he got to his feet.

'An excellent suggestion, Mr Mayor. I shall be happy to comply. If Dr Adey is still in town I shall get word back to you. And . . .' he paused and looked at Bart, 'perhaps I can arrange to have your scattered cattle recovered and kept safe until your return.'

The Reverend and Hogan departed into the night to return into the town. After they had left, Meredith suddenly gave a mighty yawn, and looked hopefully at the Hardwicks.

'You'll be wanting to rest now, Mr Mayor.' Eve Hardwick smiled. 'I've already prepared a spare room for you. The bed may be a bit small for you, but . . .'

'Thank you, madam. I am sure it will do splendidly . . . I must admit to feeling a little tired after my excursions. I will perhaps be able to discuss strategy better tomorrow.' After a grave nod to the assembly, Meredith followed the ranch-owner's wife from the living-room.

Following his ordeal the previous night, Meredith slept late, recovering his strength. The rest of the day was virtually a council of war at the Triple G. All of the various parties were keen to volunteer to be involved in the coming battle. The men from the Flying F, having had their own lives threatened, were fighting mad, and ready to follow Meredith in whatever mission he attempted. Bart's friend and fellow-rancher Bill Hardwick also insisted on joining the planned assault on Adey's mountain stronghold, together with a contingent of his own ranch hands.

'We're all set for action, Dad,' Bart said, as he, Jane, and his father sat at the table with Bill Hardwick, eating the evening meal Mrs Hardwick had set before them. 'When do we strike?'

'I propose,' Meredith said, as Hardwick's wife poured him some coffee, 'that we launch our assault party under cover of darkness tonight. Adey may believe that you and Jane are dead, but he will have learned of my escape, and has no doubt already joined his men in the mountains. I suggest that at about four hours before dawn we set off for the mountains, son.'

Bart nodded. 'A full invasion party this time?'

'Er – yes.' Meredith rubbed his chins thoughtfully and smiled at Bill Hardwick. 'We will have two "battalions" as it were – ourselves and the men of the Flying F, together with Mr Hardwick here and those of his own men who have volunteered.' Meredith beamed and then continued with his meal.

Once the meal was over, Meredith remained at the table examining the new gun Hardwick had provided for him, loaded it fully, and took care that his gun belt was also well supplied with ammunition. He raised an eyebrow as Bart's wife did the same. Jane caught his look and smiled faintly.

'Don't even dare suggest that I stay behind, Randle – or you, either, Bart!' she remarked. 'I'm coming on this trip, and that's flat. This is is my fight too, remember. Adey tried to burn me to death.' Bart smiled and gripped her hand.

'An entirely understandable sentiment, Miss Jane,' Meredith commented. 'I would suggest, however, that you both try and snatch a few hours' sleep this evening, before we depart – as I intend to do. We'll need to be as fresh as possible to keep going during the night. I will awaken you at the appropriate time.'

'Just see that you do!' Jane laughed.

'And I would advise you, and all the men, to do the same, sir,' he remarked to Bill Hardwick. 'We may run into quite a deal of trouble. Might I have you saddle a large stallion for me, Mr Hardwick? Unfortunately my own horse was left in town.'

'Sure thing,' the rancher agreed. 'Now – or later?'

'Later – when we awaken. I will awaken you at the same time as I rouse Bart and Jane.'

Hardwick departed to brief his own men, and Bart did the same for the boys of the Flying F. Bart left the room confident of the fact that if Meredith said he would awaken four hours before dawn, he would.

And he did, using his customary mental process of telling himself the exact hour to finish sleeping. Without undue disturbance he woke Bart, sleeping in a separate room with Jane; then Bill Hardwick was also aroused. He prepared the horses, whilst in the dim cold his wife fixed up provisions for them. By the time they came down the ranch-house steps, warmly clad, they found that the task force of the rest of the men was already assembled and waiting in the yard, under the supervision of foreman Kevin Briggs.

So presently they got on their way, riding into the curious violet darkness that always gathered at that time of the Arizona night.

The party struck across the pastureland, speeding through the ground-level mist, which clung about them like the fingers of a ghost. All the night wind had gone at this hour. Instead there was a deathly stillness and the immensity of sky. The stars looked dimmer, as though tired with their solitary blazing in the night. Away in the distance, gaunt and black, the mountain range flowed into the common darkness of the plain and pastureland.

They rode hard, to travel as far as possible before the daylight came. Meredith had calculated that the ride, with their horses fresh, would take two hours. By that time they ought to be in the heart of the mountains, well fixed for further activity. They could move in the mountains by day because they had ample cover; it was the approach which they did not dare risk in the light.

After a while they left the pastureland and hit the desert trail itself. It had an even more spectral aspect than the grasslands. Occasionally giant cacti loomed up, spiked and shadowy tridents, which faded and were gone. Lizards slithered quickly away from the drumming hoofs, or rats squeaked in a sudden panic. Then the nature of the arid trail changed a little as Meredith, in the lead, plunged away from it obliquely in the hope of cutting perhaps a couple of miles from the total. The small army sped through the sage, which as rapidly changed to the lance-like yuccas, dimly visible in the dark. The icy twilight, the silence, the calm – they remained unbroken save for the beat of the hoofs as mile after mile flew by.

At a spot thick with agaves Meredith called a halt and the lathered horses were given a brief rest and a drink. Bart cast an eye towards the east, and suddenly gave a start.

'Look over there,' he said, pointing. 'Isn't that a horse?'

Instantly all eyes swung in the direction Bart had indicated. There was no doubt about it. About eighty yards away was the unmistakable shape of a riderless horse.

'This may be significant,' Meredith commented. 'Get remounted – we need to get over there.'

Bart was the first to reach the horse, and as he neared the animal he caught sight of a dark shape sprawled in the grass immediately in front of it. He jumped from his saddle and bent to examine the shape, instantly confirming his suspicion that it was the body of a man. Dropping to one knee he turned the figure over gingerly.

'Hell's bells! *It's Hogan!*' he exclaimed, as the others joined him.

Hogan was unconscious. Meredith bent over him, and using his hand as a shield from the wind, struck a lucifer. The flame was quickly extinguished, but its light had lasted long enough for Meredith to ascertain that Hogan had been shot.

The bullet had struck him just below his left shoulder, and must have lodged somewhere near the heart. The bleeding alone showed that immediate attention was essential if there was to be any hope.

For anyone to take him back for medical attention would deplete their attacking force. To continue meant that the outlaw might die. Meredith looked up at the men around him.

'Any of you men got any medical knowledge?' he asked.

Bill Hardwick dismounted.

'I ain't a doctor, but I've got some knowledge of frontier doctorin'. I'll do what I can. Get a fire started to heat some water. Anyone got any medical kit?'

'I've got something in my saddle-bag,' Jane said promptly. 'Just one or two things, but I thought they might be useful.'

'I need a bottle of whiskey!' Hardwick snapped. There was a general shaking of heads, then several of the men produced small flasks. 'Guess they'll have to do,' Hardwick grunted, rolling up his sleeves.

The area used for the operation was far from ideal. Hogan lay on a flat rock, covered with coats and blankets. The only light was from their smoky oil-lanterns, casting an uncertain light.

Hardwick washed his hands with whiskey and selected a probe from the small case of instruments Jane had produced. He nodded to Bart and Meredith who were crouched either side of the unconscious outlaw.

'Right. Cut off his shirt and hold him down tightly.' He waited until they had grasped the outlaw's arms. 'If you let him move he could die.'

Carefully he probed at the wound, compressing his lips at the sight of the oozing blood. Unless he was quick he would be wasting his time. He gave a sigh as the slender probe located the bullet, then carefully he extracted the slug.

'Water!' he commanded.

Hardwick used it to sluice out the wound, held out his hand for a whiskey-flask and poured the raw spirit into the gaping wound. Hogan groaned, tried to heave upright, then relaxed as Bart and Meredith tightened their grip. Hardwick plugged the wound, then applied a crude bandage.

'If he escapes infection he might just live,' Hardwick said, wiping his hands. At his signal someone handed him another opened flask. 'Mighty lucky for Hogan that he was unconscious to begin with.' He tilted the flask, swallowed, and passed it back to one of the men. 'I needed that.'

'What are we going to do with Hogan?' Bart asked.

'He's hurt bad,' said Hardwick. 'He shouldn't be moved at all.'

'We could do with him conscious,' Meredith mused. 'I'd like to know who attacked him, and how he got here. Also, he might be able to tell us where the Reverend's body is lying.'

'The Reverend?' Bart gasped. 'What are you talking about, Dad? There's only Hogan's horse around.'

Meredith shook his head. 'It isn't Hogan's horse – it's *Peregrine*'s! Obviously Hogan's horse took fright and bolted when he was shot – it's probably miles away by now. Peregrine must have been killed too – but we don't have time to search for his body – and it'd be a pretty useless task in the dark anyway.'

'What do you think happened?' Jane asked.

'They must have been intercepted by Adey or his men leaving the town. They didn't want to risk their shots being heard, so they made them ride with them on their way to the mountains. As soon as they reached this safe distance, they were shot . . .' Meredith broke off as there came an unearthly groan from the unconscious man. He stirred with returning consciousness.

'Quiet, all of you!' Meredith snapped, and bent his head to within a few inches of Hogan's. 'Can you hear me?' he whispered urgently. 'This is Mayor Meredith. You're with friends. We found you . . .'

'I . . . I hear you, Mayor. Listen! I gotta . . . tell you . . .' his voice tailed off with anguish. Meredith waved a hand in a half-circle.

'The flask – quick!'

Meredith allowed a few drops to pass through the outlaw's parched lips. He rallied a little and began whispering. Meredith bent his ear to catch the sounds. The others, unable to hear what was being said, waited in tense expectancy.

At length Meredith stood up and carried Hogan towards his own horse. To everyone's complete amazement, he tied him to his saddle horn, then he heaved himself up into the saddle behind the outlaw's slumped figure. He supported the outlaw with one hand and grabbed the reins with the other.

'He's coming with us,' Meredith announced. 'And before you say anything, he *wants* to come with us. He knows he's risking his life, but he insisted.' He glanced up at the sky.

'We've lost time. It's nearly dawn. I want to be well into the heart of the mountains before the actual day comes. The prevalent mist will provide excellent cover.' He dug in his spurs and moved off, as the others scrambled to their own mounts.

Bart quickly caught up with his father.

'What the hell goes on, Dad? Who shot Hogan?'

117

'It was *Peregrine* who shot Hogan!' Meredith's voice was bitter with self-recrimination. 'The man's a complete fake – he's the man behind all this, the man who's been giving the orders to Adey! The cunning swine knew we might come across Hogan's horse, so he swapped his mount with it to throw us off the scent! He made a big mistake though – in his hurry to warn his friends in the mountain of our planned attack, he failed to make certain that Hogan was actually dead!'

Bart exchanged a stunned look with Jane – and with Hardwick, who was riding alongside and had heard the revelation.

'Instead of riding back into town as he told us at the Triple G, Peregrine headed for the foothills,' Meredith explained. 'He confided in Hogan, whom he expected to throw in his lot with him being an outlaw. He tried to recruit him to his gang.'

'I can guess the rest,' Bart said grimly. 'Hogan may have been a robber, but he's no killer. He'd told us as much. He must have refused the offer – so Peregrine shot him!'

'With a hidden derringer,' Meredith assented.

'Then we're riding into a trap!' Jane exclaimed in dismay.

'Forewarned is forearmed,' Meredith said calmly.

'What else did Hogan tell you?' Hardwick asked.

'Nothing yet. He's passed out, which is hardly surprising considering the pain he's in.'

Whilst it was yet dark on the trail, the day was creeping to the mountain heights – a magnificent sight. Oblique sunlight struck the eternal snows at the mountain summits and turned them to winking spires flashing a myriad iridescent colours against a violet-ebony sky. The stars paled. The mist began to writhe down below as warmer air filtered through the piercing cold of the night. Then, gradually but inexorably, the daylight slid down those sparkling peaks to the greyer regions below the snowline.

But before the torrid sun itself had come into view the party had gained the foothills and were moving along a tortuous trail which Meredith felt certain would keep them more or less concealed from all prying eyes. It was a long trail, going ever upwards, and, as near as Meredith could judge, it would lead them eventually to where he knew the cave entrance to be situated.

7

NAVAJO VENGEANCE

The small army of gun-hawks guarding the mountain entrance to the catacombs had been thinking how easily they would earn their promised huge bonuses by wiping out Meredith's forces. Peregrine's arrival the previous night – giving them ample warning of the planned raid – had enabled them to carefully plan an ambush. Lying in concealment high above the trail, they had waited for the coming slaughter.

The day had passed without incident. Complacency began to set in as the night wore on. Perhaps Meredith had chickened out of his planned attack . . . Several of the men ran true to type and dozed. It was as well for one of them that he remained alert and caught a faint sound in the stillness, which could have been the falling of a stone. It was not repeated, but the gunman looked about him warily, his .45 in his hand. Then he stood up slowly, unconscious of the fact that he made a perfect silhouette against the brilliant stars and violet sky.

Not far away a figure was standing flat against a rock, as motionless as the shadows for a moment; then he unslung something from about his neck and with his free hand reached behind him. There was a pause, then a dull twang like strong elastic flying back into shape.

The gunman never knew what happened. Tearing hell went through his chest and heart and he reeled from his perch, his body bouncing and rebounding from the rocks and crashing at last into a narrow gully. He remained motionless, the shaft of an arrow straight through his body.

The job had been done in such silence the remaining gunmen had no idea what had happened. They still snoozed on, regardless, blankets drawn around them against the chill of the night. It was only instinct that warned them of danger, for suddenly one of them sat up sharply, blinked, and looked around him. He was just in time to see half a dozen or so shadowy figures gliding towards him – then before he could speak and warn his comrades the figures hurtled forward, their steel-strong forearms closing under the chins of the men.

Knives gleamed. The Navajos slew their foes with soundless efficiency and looked as unemotional when the dead men had been tossed into the gully below as they had at the onset of their attack.

There was not one Navajo but at least two dozen, silent under the stars, all of them dressed in shirt and trousers and not in the half-naked style common to their race in the wild state. One of them, keener than the rest, stiffened suddenly and listened, pressing his ear to the ground.

'Many horses come,' he said.

'We watch,' their shadowy leader murmured. 'We do not kill yet. I have spoken.'

He jerked his head with its lankly falling black hair and

121

with his comrades retreated into the shadows. The sound of the horses' hoofs on the trail below grew nearer, then ceased. Meredith, at the head of about two dozen riders – Bart and Jane beside him – slid from the saddle of his stallion, and carefully placed Hogan on the ground, wrapped in a blanket, and propped him against a rock. Meredith glanced around him.

'Cautiously from here, men,' he advised. 'I have no means of knowing the exact spot we are looking for, but this is definitely the region where the cave must be situated in the cliff face. Come on.'

Taking a gun into each hand he led the way through the rocks at the base of the mountain. It stood alone, its sharply steep side rising up from a gully, the higher peaks looming against the violet of the sky and cutting a sawtooth line against the stars.

'Hold it!' came the voice of Hardwick suddenly, hushed as much as possible. 'I trod on somethin' back there and I'll be durned if it ain't a body— Come an' take a look!'

Immediately Meredith turned back on his tracks, Jane and Bart moving with him. In another moment they were examining the corpse with the arrow through its heart.

'Remarkable,' Meredith muttered. 'The body is still quite warm. The attack can't have been made more than a little while ago – and apparently by an Indian.'

'Looks like the work of Red Eagle to me,' Jane said shrewdly.

'But why should he do this?' Bart demanded. 'I mean – how did he know we wanted this guard out of the way? How—'

'You mean *guards*,' foreman Kevin Briggs corrected, coming up in the gloom. 'There's about a dozen bodies a bit further along. All of them have been knifed, and they sure couldn't be deader.'

Meredith straightened up slowly.

'Something decidedly strange about this, son,' he commented, glancing at Bart. 'Obviously Adey had detailed this large force of men to lie in ambush for us, after Peregrine arrived to tip him off. Now they've all been wiped out! Even though it is to our advantage, I don't like it. It may upset a lot of our own plans if Red Eagle or some other Indian is pursuing a scheme of his own. I assume it might be safe to call?'

'Try it,' Bart suggested. 'If anybody shoots, we've plenty of rock cover.'

So Meredith cupped his hands to his mouth and called with all his lung power. '*Red Eagle! Red Ea–gle* . . .'

There was no response save the echoes. The party relaxed a little and looked at one another.

'Accept things as they are and let it go at that,' Jane said, in her usual practical way. 'Where's the entrance to the catacombs?'

Bart, who had been studying the cliff face, made answer.

'That looks promising up there – that round black hole. Looks like a cave or something. Let's take a look.'

They got on the move again, climbing steadily upward, and Bart's guess proved to be right. They eventually arrived at the lofty point where the gunmen had had their perch. It was deserted, the party not observing the many keen, implacable eyes watching them from a higher point still.

'No shoot,' Red Eagle murmured to the men nearest him. 'Paleface Meredith and his son and his wife my friends. Red Eagle help them, and Red Eagle avenge . . .'

Down below Bart studied the large cave entrance and sniffed at the warm wind blowing out of it. Then he scratched his head.

'This is too easy,' he muttered. 'Something suspicious about it all.'

'Suspicious or otherwise, son, the luck is apparently on our side,' Meredith responded. 'Our next task is to get the oil-lamps from our saddle-bags, so we can explore the tunnels. Mr Hardwick,' he turned to the rancher. 'I want you and your men to stay here to guard this entrance, and to act as back-up. If we don't emerge in three hours, you'd better follow us in and see if you can finish the job.'

Within minutes, the party had obtained the necessary lamps, and returned to the cave entrance. Meredith and Bart were carrying the still figure of Hogan between them. They laid him carefully down at the side of the trail, his back propped against a rock.

Bart carefully positioned the blanket around his shoulders

'Still breathing, but he appears to have fallen asleep,' he murmured.

'Leave him to us, Mr Mayor,' Hardwick said. 'You'd best be gettin' on your way. Time's getting' on, and those Indians might come back.'

'Quite,' Meredith agreed, turning back to his stallion. 'If you are ready, men – miss, son?'

Red Eagle, above, had caught every word and he stirred a little.

'We too move,' he murmured. 'Must hurry. We go to the southern entrance in mountain foothills. Palefaces inside do not know it exists. We can surprise them. Horses wait. Come. . . .' And with his men he melted into the shadows.

Bill Hardwick and his men having been left to guard the cave entrance, Meredith, Bart and Jane, with the boys of the Flying F in their rear, were deep inside the tunnel. Oil-lamps in one hand and guns in the other, they slowly penetrated into the Stygian depths.

'Randle! Bart! Take a look at that,' Jane exclaimed, swinging her lamp towards a large slab set into the cave wall.

Holding his own lamp close to the slab, Meredith peered at a series of inscriptions chiselled into it. Bart looked over his shoulder, and the others waited interestedly.

The light from their lamps revealed a series of remarkable drawings and symbols. To Bart the whole thing was a puzzle, but evidently not to Meredith. He gave a low whistle of satisfaction.

'Discovered something?' Bart asked.

'Definitely so, son. These are the Navajo symbols Adey told me he had discovered and had translated by Peregrine. Presumably they tell of the treasures in the Halls of Manuza and threaten death to anyone trying to find them.'

They continued on their way, ready for trouble at any moment – but once again they received a complete surprise. There was not a single guard to bar their way.

'Apparently the good fairies are still on our side,' Meredith commented. 'It also suggests that the outlaws must have succeeded in completely clearing the rock barrier that Red Eagle told me his ancestors had placed here. That means that Adey and Peregrine and their men must have penetrated beyond, and may actually be in the Halls of Manuza.'

Meredith's suspicions were entirely correct. Deep inside the mountain, at the far end of the now cleared main tunnel, Peregrine and Adey, together with their remaining most trusted men – most of them carrying oil-lanterns – were about to penetrate and explore the Halls of Manuza.

'You timed your arrival nicely, Peregrine,' Adey said. 'We'd just about cleared the last rock barrier away. Now we can explore these regions together.' He peered ahead into the darkness ahead of the circle of light cast by the lamps the men carried. 'You're sure that what we'll find here will make all our efforts worthwhile?'

'Of course I'm sure,' Peregrine smiled coldly. There was an edge of barely suppressed excitement in his voice. 'The writings I translated indicated that there is a fabulous treasure hoard in here. This place is part of an old Navajo burial-ground for their tribal leaders, as well as a temple for their idols. They were known to have used silver and jewels for their images. Somewhere in here should be a sort of sacrificial stone and their idols around it. With both a sacrificial chamber *and* a burial vault involved, the treasures should be immense!'

'Unless it's already been removed,' Adey remarked.

'No chance of that,' Peregrine snapped. 'Take a look behind us. This place hasn't been entered for generations.' The party halted, and looked down at their feet. Wherever they had walked they had left deep imprints. The dust, caused by flaking from the roof above, lay densely over everything.

The slow procession continued, and there were now wolfish grins on the faces of the men. One and all, they were convinced that their fortunes were assured.

'You know, there's just one thing worrying me,' Adey said at length. 'How did that fat devil Meredith know about these Halls of Manuza? He's never seen the inscriptions at the cave entrance, and you made the only translation.'

'That's a mystery, I'll admit,' Peregrine shrugged. 'That man is certainly no body's fool – or should I say *was*. By now his party will have been ambushed and wiped out by your men when they tried to reach here. There's no way Meredith will have suspected that I rode on ahead here in time to warn you.' He smiled complacently. 'He and his helpers think I went back to town with Hogan. And *he* won't be talking to anyone. And, of course, they also believe that you won't be suspecting any attack, since you considered them dead.'

'But what if they find Hogan's body on the way here?' Adey asked shrewdly.

Peregrine laughed. 'I'd thought of that. I switched horses with Hogan. If that wise-guy Meredith finds my horse, he'll naturally assume I was killed too. He won't suspect a thing. Yes, everything has worked out nicely. By the time the townspeople pluck up the courage to come into the mountains, we'll have been long gone with the treasure.'

Adey did not answer, and the advance through the tunnel continued. The only sound was of the scuffling feet on the rough floor. More tramping for a space, then Peregrine stopped suddenly in his advance, his ear catching an unexpected sound ahead. Adey bumped into him and the men behind halted.

'What is it?' Adey questioned.

Peregrine's voice was hesitant.

'I thought I heard footfalls ahead.' He shrugged. 'Or maybe it's the echo of our own feet.'

Adey's hand dropped to his gun in the darkness.

'If it's that mug Meredith or any of his boys, we're ready for them,' he muttered. 'Bring the lamps together to give us a little more light—' He broke off with a start of alarm, and in the rear some of the men began to move in readiness for darting back down the tunnel up which they had come. For, during the brief few seconds when the light had been intensified, there was a vision of perhaps two dozen men in shirts and rough trousers, all of them dark-skinned with lank black hair and merciless faces.

'*Sweet hell – Indians!*' Adey gasped, and the lamp dropped out of his fingers. He thought of nothing else but running, having decided in that brief glimpse that the Navajos down the tunnel were out for blood. How they had got there ahead of them, what they wanted – in that moment of discovery, none of these things mattered. Instinctively they began to run back along the tunnel.

Peregrine was the first to recover from his fright. He slewed to a halt.

'Wait, you damned fools! We've got our guns! We can—'

He was wasting his breath. In those few moments, aided by their uncanny instincts and hearing, the Navajos had hurtled forward in the dark and the next thing he knew he and the men nearest to him were struggling desperately with lithe, steel-strong bodies which battered and crushed with relentless power.

The remaining men did not stop to try conclusions. They bolted into the darkness, intent on getting as far away as possible from trouble.

Peregrine, Adey, and several of the other men, however, found it impossible to escape. Their guns were taken from them and, shouting and struggling, they were forced along through the darkness, not having the slightest idea where they were going – but their general impression was that they were constantly going downwards, into the southern tunnel extensions they had never suspected existed but which were known to the Navajo whose natural ancestral habitat these catacombs were.

So, eventually, they came into an area where yellow light glowed fitfully. It proved to be a cavern of immense size into the rugged walls of which were thrust smoky torches, their wavering flames casting on to stone effigies, sacrificial slabs, and abandoned totem poles. Here evidently was some ancient Navajo temple, never discovered by white men but well enough known to the Indians.

Peregrine looked around him desperately. There were a dozen Navajos holding him and the eight men who had been brought along with him. But there were also quite a score more of Navajos in various parts of this underground temple. They sat on the stone seats or stood in the shadows, all of them utterly inscrutable and as motionless as statues.

The Navajo who had been making a particular point of holding Peregrine left his task to his comrades and strode ahead. He mounted a crude stone altar.

'Me Red Eagle,' said the figure at the altar. 'Me servant of Paleface Meredith and his son and his wife. Me not like way of you and your braves.'

'I never did anything to you!' Peregrine retorted, gathering courage as he realized this particular Indian at least was not a savage throwback to earlier times.

'You fight Merediths, so you fight Red Eagle. Red Eagle has vowed vengeance on palefaces who dared to invade the tombs of our ancestors.'

'Listen to me, Red Eagle,' Adey said, also with returning courage. 'We haven't done anything to your ancient tombs. We were simply exploring these tunnels . . .'

The dark, deadly eyes pinned the doctor steadily.

'Red Eagle not like the voice of the paleface,' he said, and made a brief signal. In consequence, Adey found himself seized even more tightly and dragged forward until he was in front of the altar.

'You enemy of my people and of the white men who are my friends.' Red Eagle announced. '*Destroy him!*'

'Wait a minute!' Adey gasped frantically, striving to tear away. '*Wait. . . !*'

He got no further. A knife flashed and gouged at him from the Navajo holding him and to Peregrine, standing a little distance away, there was the vision of Adey toppling over to the floor. His dead body was lifted and carried without ceremony from the chamber to somewhere beyond it.

'Red man have no mercy on white men he hates,' Red Eagle explained. 'All of you have been watched. You invaded these sacred regions. You came to steal treasures of our ancestors.'

'I'm afraid I did.' Peregrine knew he was in deadly danger and sought refuge through apology. 'But I didn't know these tunnels had anything sacred about them – and if I have desecrated anything, I'm humbly sorry.'

'Red Eagle not believe you. You killed whites who are the friends of Red Eagle. I gathered my comrades from far and near and we agreed we must be avenged – but not only for the things you did in Mountain Peak. To have dared to enter the Halls of Manuza is enough. My ancestors say you must die!'

'Just a minute, Red Eagle . . .' Peregrine's voice wavered. He, as an expert on Navajo history, knew the lengths to which an Indian might go when impelled by ancestral motives, and Red Eagle seemed to be consumed with all the fanaticism of his race. 'As a civilized man you should know that it is not justice to kill a man or order him to be killed without a fair trial. I swear to you I did not know I was invading sacred Navajo territory.'

'I have heard enough – and seen enough,' Red Eagle retorted, his eyes glinting. 'Your men guarded the northern door in the foothills. We dealt with them, as we shall deal with you. You took these sacred halls unto yourself, and Navajo law says the penalty for the unbidden is death.'

Peregrine started to protest again, but he did not get

the chance. He was impelled forward as far as the altar, then a violent shove sent him stumbling to his knees. His men watched in fearful silence, wondering not so much about his fate as their own.

'Red Eagle said earlier that all enemies of the whites who befriend red man are enemies of red man too. All of you here are enemies – and enemies die. So says the law. Some escaped, but they will be found. You must learn, paleface, that to invade the sacred land of the Navajo is to face death. . . .'

Red Eagle made a brief signal and then folded his arms, his face expressionless. Peregrine, all his control gone, began to shout and scream desperately for release – but none was given. Hard though he struggled, he was in the end brought level with the huge sacrificial slab in the centre of the great cavern and flung upon it.

Meredith, Bart, and the boys of his outfit were advancing steadily along the northern tunnel. Then the foreman, who had volunteered to scout ahead, came hurrying back with every evidence of urgency. He stopped at Meredith's side, breathing hard.

'There's somethin' queer, ahead Mr Mayor. I distinctly heard the voices of men comin' towards us. They didn't seem to be carryin' any lights – and I could hear them cursin' as they ran into each other. Funny thing is, they seemed to be terrified – and yellin' somethin' about Indians!'

'Remarkable,' Meredith commented, frowning. 'Why this sudden anxiety to come back? If they are aware of us, they'd surely wait quietly in the darkness to ambush us.'

'Can't see how they even know we're here, Dad,' Bart pointed out. 'Best thing we can do is to extinguish our lamps, and slip into these alcoves at the side of the tunnel until they run past. Then we can step out and nab them from behind.'

'Excellent strategy, son,' Meredith approved. He glanced at the men. 'Quickly – do as he suggested.'

Tensely, the party waited in the darkness.

'Still shoutin', Mr Mayor,' Briggs whispered. 'Listen!'

Meredith strained his ears and caught the words floating up from the depths.

'Hasn't any of you mugs kept a lamp? We've got to shift quicker than this, with those damned Indians after us. . . !'

'I've got some lucifers,' a voice muttered. There was the scrape of a match . . . then another. Perhaps a minute later, a group of men came lurching past, faintly illumined by the match their leader was holding aloft.

'You are covered from behind, my friends,' Meredith said, stepping out from the alcove. 'Stop where you are, or we shall shoot you down.' Bart and the other men re-lighted their oil-lamps and stepped out also, guns levelled in their free hands.

'I ain't interested in tryin' anything,' the man holding the match answered – then he swore luridly as the match burned down to his fingers. 'All I want is to be out of these tunnels and among white men, even if they is enemies.'

The fugitives raised their hands as the boys of the Flying F stepped forward and relieved them of their weapons.

'Kindly explain further,' Meredith ordered.

'There's a lot of stinkin' Indians down in them tunnels and they've already got the boss and Dr Adey – mebbe even killed 'em by now. We wanted to get outa here afore they caught up on us . . .'

'Are there any more of you?' Meredith questioned.

'Guess there ain't all of us here,' said the man who'd burned his fingers, looking about him. 'Some of the boys scattered down another tunnel when the Indians attacked an' I don't know where they went.'

'You say these Indians got Peregrine? Your boss?' Meredith asked sharply.

'Sure did – and Doc Adey and a bunch of the boys.'

'Where were they taken?'

'I dunno. I'd no chance to find out with it bein' dark after we dropped our lamps. I was only interested in gettin' away . . .'

'This has got to be looked into,' Meredith said abruptly, glancing at Bart and the men around him. 'It sounds to me like Red Eagle on the rampage, and he must be taught that he cannot do as he likes in these days. There are laws . . .' He pondered for a moment, then:

'Four of you keep these men covered and take them back to the tunnel entrance where Bill Hardwick and his boys are standing guard. Alert them to what's happened, and tell them to keep a sharp look-out. Better still,' he added, thinking, 'tell them to block up the entrance of the cave with stones as a precaution. If we return safely I'll call out for the barrier to be removed. If not, tell Bill and his boys to open up on whoever emerges from the cave!'

Meredith's orders were obeyed, and the men moved off.

'What now, Dad?' Bart asked. 'We go on, I suppose?'

'There's a problem,' Meredith answered, re-lighting his own lamp. 'Our scared departed friends had no idea where Peregrine and his men have been taken. However, since there seem to be very few branch tunnels – those we saw on the way in here simply led to empty chambers, which the outlaws used for sleeping and keeping their horses – I think we can assume that the opposite direction would be taken – towards the southern entrance known only to the Navajos. Let us see what we can find.'

He began advancing with the men behind him, the light from his lamp projecting a short way ahead. Following a blur of footprints in the dusty, rocky floor leading south, quite unconsciously Meredith went past the branch tunnel which led down to the temple of the Navajos and continued on his way.

He received a grim surprise as he turned a bend in the tunnel. Straight ahead of him, and only a few yards away, were the remainder of Peregrine's men who had bolted at the advent of the Navajos. Now they stood in a row with their guns levelled.

At the sight off Meredith, visible from the lamplight reflecting back from the walls, the men looked vaguely surprised for a moment but only for a moment, then the centremost snapped out an order.

'Take it easy, Fatty! Freeze right there. You'll get blasted wide open if you don't. Tell those men behind you to lower their weapons or we'll drill you.'

Meredith hesitated. He knew he had not time to level his gun, but the possibility of throwing his lamp occurred to him. Then he decided against it. No matter what he did, there were enough guns trained on him to ensure he would be hit. He called out to Bart and his men to comply.

'Get their guns, fellers,' the centremost man ordered, and advanced as he spoke. Meredith waited until the frisking was over before he said anything.

'Listen, my friend,' he said, 'I am not at the moment concerned with you and your colleagues. I am seeking Peregrine and his comrades who have fallen into the hands of Navajos.'

'As if we didn't know,' the gunman said sourly. 'Dammit, Fatty, we only just escaped from 'em. How come you're so interested in savin' Peregrine, anyways? He ain't a pal of yourn.'

'True – but he is still a white man and comes under our laws. I cannot permit the Navajos to do as they like.'

'I reckon it's one helluva slice of luck that you happened to come down here, Fatty. Me an' the boys had gotten these guns ready for the Indians if they tried to get us. If anybody can get us outa this blasted tunnel you can. You can get movin' to the foothill entrance. I expect you've got men there, but with you and these other mugs as hostages we should be able to get clear.'

'I tell you I have to find Peregrine!' Meredith insisted.

'The hell with him: we just want out. Anyways, we don't know where he is, or those red devils, either. Now get movin' back along the tunnel!'

Cornered, Meredith could do nothing else but move, the others following. Eventually the closed entrance in the face of the foothill cliff came into view, the beam from the lamps revealing it clearly.

'OK. Start yellin' and get your outside men to shift them stones!' the leading gunman ordered. Meredith glanced at him in the dim light.

'I'm warning you, my uncouth friend, that once you put your face beyond this opening you will be shot down.'

'Let me worry about that. If I go down, so do you.'

Meredith compressed his lips, then megaphoning his mouth he shouted:

'Hey, out there! Meredith speaking! Clear a space in the rocks!'

A dim voice floated from the other side.

'That you, Mr Mayor? Your voice ain't distinct. Can you prove it?'

'My compliments on your caution,' Meredith shouted, then reeled off the names of Hardwick, Jane and some others.

'Good enough for me,' came the voice from the other

side, and immediately there came the sound of rocks being moved away.

After a few minutes, when a small opening had appeared at one side of the entrance, the leading gunman said sharply:

'Tell him to stop out there, Fatty. I ain't takin' no chances. You first,' the gunman ordered.

Meredith gave a wry smile. 'I don't think my ample girth can get through that small opening.'

'Don't hand me that! I ain't riskin' going through there without bein' right behind you with a gun. Start tryin'! If you can't do it, then the whole lot's gotta be shifted.'

Meredith shrugged, then went on his knees and pushed his head and shoulders through the gap. When he got as far as his waist he stuck solid. The men outside and Jane looked at him in vague amazement. Hogan was slumped sitting to one side, his back against a rock, apparently unconscious.

'What gives, Mr Mayor?' asked Bill Hardwick, leaning forward.

'Not me anyway,' Meredith panted drily, unconscious of the weird figure he cut jammed in the hole with his Homburg aslant over one eye. 'I would appear to be nipped in the bud – but that is in keeping with my strategy.'

'Yeah?' Hardwick repeated blankly, glancing at his men. 'Ain't no use you tryin' to get out that way. We can soon push aside the rest of the rocks, and—'

'Listen to me,' Meredith interrupted. 'Behind me in the tunnel are a flock of Peregrine's armed men. They have the drop on Bart and the boys. They cannot hear what I am saying to you because my body blocks the hole. Scatter for safety, all of you, the moment you've cleared a wider space for us to come through. I am being used as a hostage to let these men of Peregrine's get away clear. That won't happen if you go to the end of the hard-sand trail, conceal yourselves above somewhere, and cover the men as they attempt to depart. Better take Hogan with you, too, if he's still alive. I'll look after myself . . . You understand?'

'Sure – but how come you got yourself hog-tied? What goes on?'

'Navajos,' Meredith answered ambiguously, then he gasped and winced a little as he received a resounding kick on his rear from inside the tunnel. He began to squirm backwards and at last stood up, straightening his Homburg.

'You been up to somethin', Fatty?' demanded the gunman suspiciously.

'I was just instructing my men to move more rocks. There is obviously no other way for a man of my dimensions.'

Tensely the parties waited whilst more rocks were moved aside. Beyond, there became visible the hard-sand clearing surrounded by rocks, but there was no evidence of any men.

'All right,' the gunhawk muttered, jerking his .45. 'Out you go, Fatty. One false move outa you and it'll be your last.'

Meredith walked forward, his hands raised. The men outside had followed his instructions: there wasn't a sign of them anywhere.

'Somethin' fishy about this,' the gunman said, when the rest of his comrades had emerged. 'I think this fat guy is tryin' to pull somethin' . . .'

Meredith was silent, wondering which way the cat was going to jump – and as he had expected, after some moments the gunman started moving down the hard-sand trail, because there was no other way he could go. His men trailed behind him, their guns ready, Meredith and his own party in the midst of a close-packed circle.

By the time the end of the hard-sand trail had been reached without incident, the gunhawks seemed to have gathered more confidence.

'I reckon it's a good idea keepin' an important guy as a hostage,' the leader commented. 'Even if we're bein' watched there ain't much anybody can do whilst I've got a bead on the guy. We should—'

'Pardon me, sir,' Meredith interrupted. The gunman glanced at him sourly.

Suddenly Meredith slammed out a straight right with perfect timing. The gunhawk had never expected such a move whilst he had his revolver in his hand and his men around him with their hardware ready. The blow had all Meredith's immense weight behind it and it knocked the man clean over.

'*Now!*' Meredith yelled. 'Pile into 'em, boys. It's our only chance. We'll get help from above.' At his shout the men who were concealed higher up the pass came into action. They hurtled out of their hiding-places, guns blazing, and the guns of Peregrine's men fired back.

Meredith hurtled at the gunman he had knocked over, snatched his .45s, and then swung round, firing first one and then the other as he came under fire himself. One bullet took a piece out of his arm and made him grit his teeth – another whanged his Homburg from his head and he forgot himself far enough to swear.

Out of the confusion a certain pattern took shape as one lot of men fled to the rocks for cover and the others climbed up higher so they could snipe downwards. Meredith recovered his Homburg as a bullet exploded in the dust in front of his hand, then holding his wounded arm he dived behind a rock-spur and spent a second or two recovering his breath.

'I reckon this is just a shootin' match, Mr Mayor,' the man beside him said. 'Whoever runs outa bullets first'll be the loser.'

'Which is enough for me,' Meredith muttered. 'I want you men to keep these gunhawks busy whilst I slip back into the tunnel. I've got to locate Peregrine. I consider him my personal responsibility . . .' He removed his jacket, then with his free hand ripped his shirt-sleeve and twisted it into a rough bandage about his arm.

'Bad, Mr Mayor?'

'I think not. Torn flesh, but no bullet. I ought to lower my blood-pressure, anyway . . . Now, you know what to do?'

'Sure thing . . .'

A .45 in his hand, the other in its holster, Meredith crept away from behind the spur and used the rocks behind it for cover. The gunmen he left behind were so intent on spitting hell at each other they did not notice him: in fact, they hardly could unless they were at a higher level. So he gained the tunnel again. Picking up one of the many discarded oil-lanterns, he hurried into the depths.

7

THE FANGS OF MANUZA

It was a curious sound that finally arrested Meredith's attention. At first it was only a whisper caught by the rocky galleries around him, but after a while it changed to a distinct chanting, becoming clearer as he hurried on – then as he crossed the tunnel down which Peregrine had been taken, he heard the sound clearly. It obviously came from many male throats, sounding very much like the incantations of a ceremonial.

Meredith hurried on, his Homburg on the back of his head, blood drying on his injured arm, then as he came suddenly on the giant ceremonial cavern of the Indians he stopped dead. The scene before him looked as though it had been transplanted from a page in history.

Peregrine – for there was no doubt it was he – was stretched out flat on the huge sacrificial slab, bound tightly to it. Around him a file of Indians was moving solemnly, chanting as they went, whilst on the altar over-looking the scene Red Eagle stood in imperturbable calm.

Against a further wall, all of them bound immovably, were the remainder of Peregrine's men.

Meredith blundered into the cavern, his gun at the ready, shouting as he moved.

'Red Eagle, stop this business immediately! Have you taken leave of your senses?'

The Indian raised his hand and it was sufficient to stop the ceremony. The Navajos waited, their hard, dark eyes fixed on Meredith as he stumbled forward. Peregrine's eyes rolled round in sudden hope.

'Meredith,' he panted, 'Get me out of this! I'll fight a battle with any man, but not with these savages. They've already knifed Adey where he stood!' Meredith ignored him and looked at the implacable Indian as he gazed down from the altar, his arms folded.

'Red Eagle friend of Paleface Meredith,' the Navajo said, 'but Red Eagle not like interference in ritual. Our law says this white invader must die, and those who came with him.'

'Kill him, and you put me in a terrible fix,' Meredith insisted. 'I have to account for him to the white man's law. Would you satisfy your own revenge and leave me to take the blame? If so, Red Eagle, you have changed.'

'Red Eagle know only law of his tribe.' The dark eyes were becoming malevolent. 'Red Eagle finding it hard to stay as friend to Paleface Meredith.'

It dawned on Meredith that this was not Red Eagle, the tight-lipped and usually speechless servant of the Flying F: he had reverted to type, as many of his race had done before him, and all the veneer of the white man's civilization had gone.

'Release that man!' Meredith commanded, abruptly changing his tactics and pointing his gun deliberately at the Indian. 'Since you won't listen to reason, Red Eagle, you leave me only the alternative of force.' None of the Navajos budged, and certainly Red Eagle did not move. His arms remained folded and his face was as frozen as an image.

'Red Eagle leave decision to the gods,' he said at last. Then, clapping his hands sharply together he added, 'Fetch the Fangs of Manuza!'

One of the Navajos departed into one of the adjacent caverns and Meredith waited, holding his aching arm and feeling a trickle of blood starting anew. He was racking his brains to try to remember something about the Fangs of Manuza. Somewhere he had read of them, but. . . ?

Then the Navajo who had been dispatched returned. On a thin sheet of stone, shaped like a tray, he was carrying what looked to be two huge ivory fangs, deeply yellow. One, at the broadest part – the root – was darkly stained as if with blood. The other was unblemished. Red Eagle took them and held one up in each hand with a good deal of unnecessary ceremony.

'The Fangs of Manuza decide,' he said. 'In the days when our race ruled this territory, before the coming of the pestilential white man, these fangs were drawn from a living creature and our race has since obeyed their will.' Looking at the fangs, Meredith wondered if they were prehistoric. Sabre-tooth tigers had once inhabited parts of America in the dim past.

'You, Paleface Meredith, have asked the gods for a decision through me,' Red Eagle said. 'I shall obey whatever the gods command. Take a fang in each hand and turn your back. You may move the fangs from hand to hand as you wish before you face me again. If I draw the one that is white, then my dictate shall be carried through. If I draw the other, the gods have favoured you and I shall do as you command. I have spoken.'

142

'A moment,' Meredith said slowly. 'You mean you will do everything I command if you draw the one that is tarnished?'

'Yes. Take the fangs.'

Meredith took one in each hand and then turned his back as ordered, so that he faced the distant opposite cavern wall. Peregrine watched anxiously, and so did his men. Upon this one slender chance, it seemed, depended their only hope of ever staying alive. Meredith's shoulders were visible, moving a little as he switched from hand to hand. From the back view he cut a weird figure in his torn shirt, Homburg on the back of his head, blood still trickling slightly down his injured arm.

'Turn!' Red Eagle commanded.

Meredith obeyed, the untainted tip of each Fang standing up out of either hand. Red Eagle was motionless for a long moment, then he reached down from the altar and made his choice, removing a stained fang and considering it.

'I win, Red Eagle,' Meredith said quietly.

The Navajo hesitated, then his primitive faith in the decision mastering him he straightened a little.

'The gods have chosen,' he said. 'Return the twin fangs.'

'I'll return it when you've had Peregrine and his men released. I don't trust you any more, Red Eagle, after this.'

Red Eagle motioned with his hand.

'Release them!'

Set-faced, the Indians obeyed. Meredith moved across to Peregrine to make sure the job was done thoroughly, and then he watched as the gunmen were released. Satisfied at length Meredith returned, and handed over the twin fangs. The Indian regarded them unemotionally and placed them on the stone tray. A mere motion of his head was sufficient to send his Navajo colleague into the adjoining chamber, tray in his hand.

'Enemies we might be, Meredith, but this is one thing I've got to thank you for,' Peregrine said.

Meredith just gave him a cold stare, then turned and looked at Red Eagle. 'I am relying on you, Red Eagle, to obey my orders,' he said. 'Dispatch these Navajo friends of yours to wherever you found them. Come to the Flying F when it is rebuilt and return to your normal duties – and bring your wife with you. If you do that, nothing further will be said about this incident – not by me, at least. If you do not, I shall be compelled to have you hunted down and turned over to the white man's law. The days when Navajos practised their ceremonies are over . . . even down here in this ancient ceremonial hall.'

Red Eagle was silent, his black eyes smouldering, but as he was fanatical in one direction, so he was in another.

'Red Eagle obey,' he muttered, and then he swung on his men and dismissed them. They filed out, apparently stolidly accepting the decision that had been forced upon them.

Meredith heaved a sigh as they vanished from the chamber.

'Now, my friends, kindly walk ahead of me – all of you. I warn you that even if I am damaged in one arm, I can still use the hand.'

The men looked at the two guns Meredith was firmly holding and decided not to argue. They began marching, but they did not proceed very far. When they came to the opening of the cavern they discovered the way barred, not by rock but by a vast door of dark-red metal that could have been copper. Upon it was engraved all manner of weird symbols.

'What the hell's this?' one of the gunmen demanded,

144

whirling around in the light of the flickering wall torches. 'I never heard the Indians pull this across!'

Meredith shrugged. 'Possibly this door is used quite a deal by the Navajos who come here via their secret entrance. Note the base of it.'

Peregrine and his men stooped to look and saw now that the door had been slid along a well-lubricated slot. When not in use it evidently fitted into a section of the rock.

'Can't budge the damned thing,' one of the men panted, tugging at it. 'Those Navajo have tricked us after all.'

'This may explain Red Eagle's occasional attacks of wanderlust,' Meredith mused. 'A door like this points to something of extreme value being somewhere down here, sealed from the pryings of the white man—'

'To hell with that!' one of the gunmen snapped. 'How do we get out?'

'Not this way, obviously,' Meredith said. 'We had better look for another way out. For the moment we shall have to forget we are enemies and search with a common purpose.'

They began moving, looking around them on the rocky walls with the torches slowly burning down, the flickering glow casting on the weird Navajo markings. Since there were only two chambers leading off this main one they were promptly explored. In the first one were all manner of queer effigies, together with the tray of fangs, and one or two sarcophagi relating to long-dead Navajo leaders.

But in the second chamber it was different. Meredith led the way into it, his lamp in his hand. Now he stood on the threshold of the chamber with the other men around him, staring at something he could not quite believe.

'For the love of Pete, it's solid silver!' one of the

gunmen gasped. 'Say, boss, can you figure just how much that thing's worth?'

Peregrine did not reply. He was gazing at a gigantic image, all of twenty feet in height, and flawlessly carved. The lantern reflected back a dull glimmer from the metal of which the image was made, and the eyes flashed a thousand iridescent fires.

'Yes,' Meredith breathed, fascinated. 'It *is* silver, and those eyes are diamonds, or precious stones of some kind.' Then the heavy silence that fell was broken as the gunmen rushed forward to more closely study this masterpiece of wealth and sculpture.

'If this thing could be moved,' Peregrine said presently, 'it would represent a fortune in money. It's just what I hoped to find here!'

'I am aware of it.' Meredith turned a cold glance on him. 'But this image happens to be on Mountain Peak Territory, my friend, and therefore belongs to that territory. This object is obviously something from Navajo history, a god of fabulous value, but to the Navajos themselves just something to worship. Yes, indeed, I can picture now where Red Eagle came when he left the Flying F for long spells at a time. He evidently came to do his devotions.'

'Any mug wastin' his time bowin' to this thing when it can put him on velvet is plain loco,' one of the men said flatly. 'And why are we kowtowin' to this fat guy, boss? We've got him outnumbered six to one! I reckon we oughta do somethin' now we've found this idol, and—'

The gunman broke off as a voice suddenly spoke. It was the recognizable voice of Red Eagle with its deep bass tone.

'White men love silver.'

The words echoed weirdly and were evidently spoken

from a natural megaphone amidst the rocks, some concealed spot from where Red Eagle, and probably his comrades, could watch what was going on.

'White men love silver,' the voice continued. 'Justice say that white men die with silver. It will make the gods smile to know that white men have much silver and yet must die with it. I have spoken.'

The voice ceased. Possibly it had come from somewhere in the roof, since it was a mass of rough rock with many blackly yawning niches, quite inaccessible from below.

'Red Eagle is running true to tradition.' Meredith said. 'He is obviously possessed of all the subtle cruelty of his race. What worse punishment could there be than to have this silver idol, worth a fortune, and yet be unable to use it? To have to die beside it . . .'

'We're not dead yet,' Peregrine said. 'Let's keep looking for a way out— As to this idol, I'll make damned sure that you and Mountain Peak are not having it, Meredith . . .'

Peregrine stopped. There was a queer sound in the chamber, rather like the escape of air from a tyre. It grew more intense as the seconds passed and then suddenly burst forth in all its power. From one corner of the rocky ceiling water was surging down in ever-increasing volume. Meredith stared at the column, already sweeping along the dust of the floor, reflecting back the lamplight.

'The dirty skunk!' one of the men yelled. 'He's floodin' us out!'

'I hardly thought he would refer to our deaths without making them certain,' Meredith commented. 'Red Eagle, better than anybody, must know of countless underground streams which can be tapped and released – like this one!'

As he spoke Meredith hurried into the adjoining giant chamber, then he pulled up short. The torches flickering

147

on the walls showed that water was also pouring in here from two sources high in the ceiling. Evidently the underground was ready prepared for any such contingency as this.

'What the hell do we do?' Peregrine demanded, gripping Meredith's arm. 'This water isn't escaping – it's already up to our ankles! If it keeps going on—'

' 'Course it'll go on!' one of the assembled men yelled. 'We're goin' to be drowned like blasted rats!' The man's fear and fury overwhelmed him at that moment and he dived forward, intent on seizing Meredith by the throat.

Meredith fired point blank and with a howl of pain the man dropped face down in the water. He writhed and gurgled for a moment or two and then became still.

'Anyone else like to try conclusions with me?' Meredith asked, both guns now levelled and his lamp tossed away.

'All of us to just him!' one of the men panted. 'What's stoppin' you, boss? If we ever get out, he's gotten us nailed with that hardware.'

Meredith was silent, the water now swirling round his knees. Peregrine seemed set to ignore his followers' urgings – until he suddenly lashed out his left fist. Not expecting it, Meredith took the blow on the side of the face and stumbled. Instantly the rest of the men were on top of him.

There were so many of them he did not stand a chance. His revolvers were torn out of his hands and with the blind ferocity of vindictiveness Peregrine's men pushed his head and shoulders into the swirling waters. Believing their doom was inevitable the gunhawks were intent on only one thing – revenge on the man they considered had brought them into this trap.

Meredith gulped and spluttered as he came up for air – then again he was pushed under. He was preparing to die, when a clanging and rattling smote his ears in the few seconds he was allowed to come up to the air again.

At the same moment the relentless hands fell away from him and there came an abrupt staccato of revolver shots. Reeling dizzily, his damaged arm smarting from contact with the water, and his lungs aching, Meredith peered across the cavernous space. The great coppery door had been flung aside. Through the opening were streaming a party of men. In the forefront he recognized Bart, and behind him were several of his outfit.

The how and why did not concern Meredith at that moment. He was conscious of only two things – the water was rapidly pouring away now the door had been opened, and his own life was no longer in danger. Peregrine and his men were standing motionless, their hands raised.

'Good job we happened on you like we did,' Bart remarked, and then turned to stare contemptuously at Peregrine and his dishevelled men. 'Get moving, the whole stinking lot of you. Boys, keep your eye on them while I see to my father.'

Apparently Meredith had recovered from his manhandling. He retrieved his saturated Homburg from the fast-ebbing water and put it on his head; then realizing his guns were not needed any more he did not trouble himself to recover them.

'You OK, Dad?' Bart asked anxiously.

'I fancy so, son, though I did have a rough five minutes.' He beamed at his son affectionately. 'I admit I'm at a loss to understand how you arrived so opportunely.'

'Easily explained, Dad – and you can thank Jane for it! We eventually got the better of them boys out on the hard-sand trail, because they ran out of ammunition before we did. Right now they're hog-tied out there with Hardwick and the rest of the boys left to guard 'em. As we were seeing to them, Jane suddenly happened to spot a line of horsemen apparently riding out of the side of the mountain. She realized it must have been Red Eagle and his braves hightailing it from the southern entrance.'

'Bless the girl,' Meredith murmured. 'She reminds me of your dear departed mother.'

Bart grinned, enjoying the rare praise.

'I figured that if I came through that southern entrance with some of the boys, we could effect a pincer movement. Now that we knew where it was, we rode straight over to the tunnel, left our horses outside, and ran inside to find out what had happened to you. Next thing we knew we heard water gushing from somewhere, otherwise we might have searched 'til doomsday. We tracked it down to an undammed stream on the higher cavern level. We could see through cracks in the rocks what was below us – this lighted cavern I mean – so we hurried to find a way in. That brought us to the door there. Shifting the bar that was holding on the outside it didn't take two seconds. You're a lucky man, Dad. I guess even you didn't stand much chance against all those mugs – though I see you've been giving a good account of yourself.' He nodded to a waterlogged corpse floating in the shallow water.

'Quite. A fact of which I was painfully aware from the start. Quite a few things have befallen me . . . You say Jane saw Red Eagle and his braves riding away, escaping to the south?'

'That's right. We'd never catch them now.'

'So be it.' Meredith shrugged his huge shoulders. 'Let's get back to the north tunnel entrance and rejoin Bill Hardwick and the rest of our boys.'

Bart nodded and he and Meredith left the cavern, the water still pouring into it, but escaping as fast as it fell now the sealing door was pulled wide.

'I shall not forget your helping me in a crisis, men,' Meredith said, as they rejoined Bart's men waiting outside, their guns trained on Peregrine and his men. 'There is a great reward in that cavern we have just left, or rather next door to it.'

'Reward? I didn't notice anything,' Kevin Briggs said.

'You hardly would, but you have my assurance there is something in there, that, in due course, will amply compensate you and the rest of the townsfolk for your recent ordeals. . . .'

As the procession of captors and captives passed along the tunnel, Meredith came up behind Peregrine. The bogus cleric gave a gasp of pain as Meredith suddenly twisted his left arm his back. Meredith gave a second vicious twist.

'Damn you, Meredith!' Peregrine panted. 'You've got me, haven't you? You don't have to torture me!'

'That depends on you, Peregrine,' Meredith said amiably. 'I want to know how you managed to fool me, how and why you came here. You *are* the brains behind everything, aren't you? The man who translated the inscriptions? *Start talking*!' Again he twisted the man's arm, and the pain was excruciating.

'Stop it! *Stop it*!' Peregrine gasped. 'I'll tell you. When Adey discovered the cave by accident and sent me the inscriptions, I realized the possibilities of the place. I recruited Adey and others to help me. Adey's scientific knowledge in constructing gliders and mounting gas attacks helped to create the atmosphere of fear and mystery needed to keep the people away from the mountains whilst the tunnels were dug clear.'

'Had you had only the somewhat cloddish inhabitants of Mountain Peak to deal with you might have succeeded in your schemes,' Meredith commented. 'Science can be a

151

very powerful weapon when introduced into the back-woods. To me,' he continued, 'the most annoying aspect of the business is that I correctly suspected you right at the outset. But then you managed – with the help of chance – to deflect my suspicions away from you and on to Adey, who is equally implicated.'

'But this doesn't make sense!' Bart protested. 'You and Hogan saved my wife and me when our ranch was fired by Adey!'

'Yes – but that was an act I performed without the knowledge of Adey. I did it with only one object, to reas-sure you – and therefore all the people around you, which in time would have embraced the townspeople – that I had nothing to do with the business. You swallowed that notion wholesale, as I hoped you would, and switched your atten-tion to Adey. It didn't signify my rescuing you on that occa-sion, since I intended to deal with you later in any case.'

'And what if we had nailed Adey?'

'Even if he had been caught I could have handled the situation myself. By then he had already served his purpose.'

'And where does Hogan fit in?' Bart demanded.

'I'm afraid he doesn't any more. He was useful in so far as he looked like a convert to my supposed Gospel, but later he became a nuisance when he refused to throw his lot in with me. So I eliminated him.'

'That's where you're – *ouch*!' Bart gave a gasp of pain as Meredith suddenly elbowed him in the ribs.

'Sorry, son,' Meredith murmured. 'I must have stood on your toes in the dark . . .'

Bart scowled, then it dawned in him that his father did not want Peregrine to know that Hogan was still alive – though for the life of him he could not see *why*.

The cave entrance was presently reached and Meredith

and the men blinked as they emerged into the early morning sunlight. Smiling broadly, Hardwick and his men came forward and congratulated them. They brought ropes and cords with them, and the cowed outlaws were seized. Their hands bound behind them, they were shoved over to a side of the trail where a disconsolate group of their fellows was already similarly bound and guarded.

Meredith moved across and grabbed Peregrine by the arm as Hardwick was about to secure him with the others.

'Let me have a spare gun,' he requested. 'I'll take personal charge of Peregrine myself.' Hardwick shrugged and handed a weapon over. Meredith jammed the barrel in Peregrine's back and spun him round to face in another direction from where the outlaws were gathered.

'I'd like you to meet someone, Peregrine,' Meredith murmured, nudging him forward. A few yards away, sitting with his back resting on a blanket up against a rock, was the figure of "Hold-up" Hogan, now very much awake and staring intently at the cave entrance.

Suddenly Peregrine caught sight of him, and gave a visible start.

'*Hogan! But – but you're dead!*'

'Correction,' Hogan rasped, his face wreathed in a hideous smile. 'I ain't dead – *but you are!*' His right hand came up holding a gun. A shot crashed out.

A third eye suddenly blossomed low down on Peregrine's forehead as Hogan's shot took him clean between the eyes. Slowly he toppled forward, then jerked like a marionette as a second shot ripped into his chest.

A third shot whanged into the ground as Hogan's aim wavered and he slowly toppled sideways, the smoking gun still gripped in his fingers.

For a long moment, everyone remained frozen with

shock and surprise. Not so Meredith. Smiling grimly, he moved forward and dropped to one knee beside the slumped outlaw. Gently he prised the gun from his fingers and raised Hogan's head and shoulders. The outlaw stirred for a moment and opened his eyes. Recognition flickered as he stared glassily at Meredith.

'Thanks, Mr Mayor,' he whispered. 'I ain't a killer, but ... but I *had* to do that, afore ... afore I ...' his voice faded into a death rattle, and his head slumped to one side.

Meredith stood up and turned. He saw that Bart had been the first to recover from the shock of events, and was bending over Peregrine, feeling for a pulse. The rest of the men began to stir and move forward, murmuring amongst themselves with astonishment.

'Is he dead?' Meredith asked briefly.

'Completely,' Bart said carefully. He was recalling the nudge in the tunnel. 'Shot through the head – and the heart. What about Hogan?'

'I'm afraid he's dead too. An estimable gentleman indeed! I shall personally see to it that he is buried with due ceremony in the cemetery at Mountain Peak.'

Jane came forward, an accusing frown on her face.

'You planned for that, didn't you Randle? I saw you deliberately lead him over to where Hogan was sitting.'

Meredith shrugged and smiled innocently. 'You may *think* that, Miss Jane. I cannot say – except to say that our erstwhile outlaw friend has certainly paid his debt to society by saving the cost of a trial ...' He turned to Bill Hardwick.

'We have also been saved the cost of a trial for the unspeakable Dr Adey, for which we are indebted to our Navajo friends. You'll find his body – along with others – back in the tunnels. Perhaps some of your men can arrange to have them removed before we move away? The Halls of Manuza are, after all, sacred ground. There are also some horses to collect from the southern entrance . . .'

Jane's look of disapproval had turned to concern as she suddenly noticed that Meredith was gripping his arm and wincing slightly.

'Randle!' she exclaimed. 'You're hurt!'

'Slightly,' he conceded. 'All in the line of duty. Now that the excitement is over, I have become somewhat more aware of it. A bandage and dressing would not come amiss – provided you are prepared to treat someone of whom you appear to disapprove?' he said drily.

Jane tried – and failed – not to smile.

It was several hours later. Meredith's 'battalions' had returned to town, where the surviving outlaws were placed under lock and key. A telegraph message had been sent to Phoenix, outlining enough of the events to get the authorities interested.

Once the townsfolk had learned the facts, everyone was dragged off to be toasted and lionized in the Painted Lady saloon.

Meredith had eventually managed to extricate himself, pleading his injury, and had retired to his mayor's office, accompanied by Bart and Jane.

'There's nothing more for you to do, Dad,' Bart insisted, as they relaxed in the office. 'Everybody is roped in and Phoenix is a higher authority than you are. They'll do the rest. Everything will be taken care of.'

'On the contrary, son. I have not yet accounted for Red Eagle and his fellow-tribesmen. When I referred to certain things having befallen me, back in the Halls of Manuza, I meant the machinations of Red Eagle.'

'When are we going to get the full story?' Bart asked, and Jane looked on interestedly.

'Yes, what about him?' But Meredith refused to be drawn.

It was not until two weeks later that the full facts emerged. The Flying F had been rebuilt – the entire population of the town gladly volunteering their labour – and the morning sun was blazing across the yard. The cattle had all been recovered and herded back safely into the corrals, all the men of the outfit were back at work, Kevin Briggs directing them in the distance.

'And that, son, is what happened,' Meredith said, as he, Bart and Jane sat on the porch, watching the proceedings. 'I am afraid that Red Eagle reverted to type and that we shall never see him again. In many ways that is a pity: he was an excellent servant, and his wife a splendid cook.'

'Talking of the devil . . .' Jane said, and nodded in surprise across the yard.

Meredith looked, and even his urbanity was shaken for once – for coming towards them was none other than Red Eagle himself. He advanced slowly in the bright sunlight, hands at his sides, his head bent a little forward. Meredith waited, his round face grim.

'Red Eagle ready to die with ancestors,' the Navajo said, when at last he had come up to the trio. 'Red Eagle forgot the laws of the white man and became red man – for a brief hour.'

'What you really mean is you lost your head and tried to murder my father,' Bart snapped. 'I'm handing you over to the law, Red Eagle. You were a damned fool to ever come back.'

'Red Eagle sorry,' the Navajo said deliberately, quite

incapable of showing emotion even now. 'Red Eagle willing to die with ancestors for what he has done. Even by
own hand if Paleface Meredith wish it. Red Eagle not
release water into cavern: that was work of followers. I
tried to stop them. I tried to obey orders as the Fangs of
Manuza willed it.' There was silence for a moment, then
Red Eagle added:

'My comrades left me when I told them I was angered.
They have gone. I came back here, willing to die for the
thing that was done.'

'Get inside the ranch, Red Eagle, and fix me a breakfast,' Meredith said briefly. 'Is your wife with you?'

'She returned from hiding-place with me, and awaits
my fate.' He nodded to outside the gate where there were
two horses, a Navajo woman seated on one, holding the
reins of the other.

'Then bring her inside too and tell her to do her best
cooking for all of us. We need it.' Something like a gleam
of pleasure came into the Navajo's black eyes, then faded
again. He turned away with a face of teak.

The Navajo returned with his wife, and without speaking they dismounted and went into the ranch house.
Presently Bart glanced at Meredith as he went down from
the porch and started to gather the horses together
preparatory to taking them to the stable.

'You're a fool, Dad,' Bart said flatly. 'After what Red
Eagle tried to do he has no right to go free. Whenever the
mood seizes him he'll do the same thing again.'

'I think not, son,' Meredith responded, his voice quiet.
'He was carried away by fanaticism – a thing you cannot
help in a man of his calibre. I cannot altogether enforce a
punishment, because he has brought so much benefit. But
for him that silver idol I mentioned to you might never
have been found. The reward offered by the government

for that alone will be of immense benefit to our community and leave plenty over.'

'Mmm . . . true,' Bart admitted. 'But even so—'

'Besides, son, for me to stand in judgement on Red Eagle would be too much like the pot calling the kettle black. You see, when Red Eagle gave me the two ivory fangs to hold I knew that only a stained one could save my life, so whilst my back was turned – as I was ordered – I rubbed the clean one in the still-wet blood on my arm, trusting it would looked stained enough in the uncertain light to satisfy Red Eagle when he made his selection. As it happened, he chose the fang that was naturally stained, but I had so arranged it that I could not lose either way. I hazarded that in that dim yellow light the difference in colour between new blood and old would not be noticeable. I had to use that strategy to save my life.'

'But – surely he found out?' Jane asked in astonishment.

'He would have done, only I managed to retain the second fang long enough to wipe it clean again, whilst I apparently watched the untying of Peregrine and his men. A simple little strategy, son, by which I ensured my right to go on living and make Red Eagle obey me. So, you see, I can hardly act as his judge and jury now, can I?'

Bart scratched his head, then grinned.

'And he's apologizing to you!' he exclaimed.

'Just so, son. One of those little incidents, which bring a smile to the most tired face . . . Now, if you will pardon me, I will put the horses in the stable. After that, I must write a letter.'

To whom?' Jane asked in wonder.

'My Boston hatters. I am afraid that, owing to its immersion in water, my Homburg is now far too small.'

Bart and Jane saw what he meant as he went towards the stables. The famous hat only just covered the top of his head as he led the horses away . . .

R